THE OTHER BILLIONAIRE BROTHER

KRISTA LAKES

ABOUT THIS BOOK

The man I love is getting married. And it isn't to me.

I've been in love with Jonathan for as long as I can remember. I loved him as a girl. I loved him as a teenager. I loved him as an adult. I love him still.

But he doesn't love me. How could he? He's a billionaire and I'm just the butler's daughter. But when I attend a party in my Gucci dress and fancy heels, he sees me in a whole new light.

And it couldn't have come at a worse time. His high-powered wedding is in two weeks.

It falls to his older brother, Christopher, to protect Jonathan from himself. As always. And this time, that means spiriting me away and tempting me with my dream job on a tropical island.

Here, I learn that Christopher is so much more than I ever gave him credit for. He gets me in a way no man ever has. His body completes me in ways I didn't even know possible. And the way he looks at me makes me think he could be the one.

I've always been in love with Jonathan, but now that I've been with Christopher, I find I can't choose. Some people go their whole lives without finding one love of their life. Now I have to decide between two.

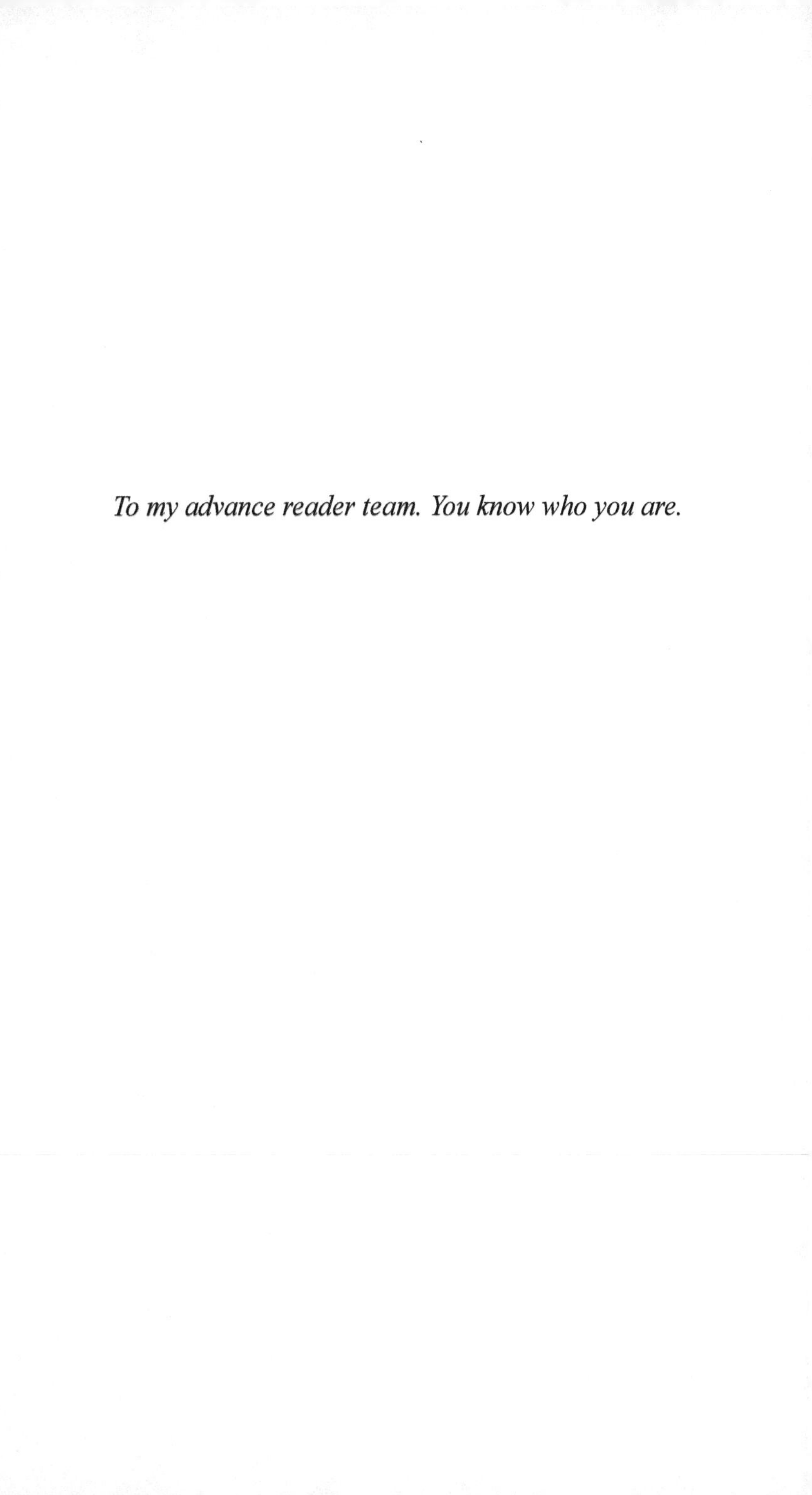

To my advance reader team. You know who you are.

CHAPTER 1

The man I love is getting married.
And it isn't to me.
I've been in love with Jonathan Lewis for as long as I can
remember.
I loved him as a girl.
I loved him as a teenager.
I loved him as an adult.
I love him still.
But he doesn't love me.
In fact, I'm fairly sure he doesn't remember I exist.

"Something's wrong," Julie says.

"What?" I glance about, concerned and looking for something out of place. I don't see anything particularly wrong. I'm just sitting on the beach with a paper plate full of fruit like I always do after work. But, as Julie was my coworker up until an hour ago, I'm afraid she's going to tell me that there was something wrong with my job performance.

She motions to the plate resting on my knees. "Something's wrong, isn't it? You've been here for ten minutes and you've barely eaten anything." She frowns at me and then inspects the plate a little closer. "And you haven't eaten your mango. You *never* have uneaten mango."

I look down at my plate and see that she's right. There's still half of a mango among the other fresh fruits. I've barely eaten anything, which, given that I love to eat, is definitely strange.

"I'm just distracted," I say with a shrug.

"Are you nervous about the flight home? The conference?" Julie asks, sitting down in the warm sand beside me. The Caribbean sun is just starting to set, turning the turquoise blue waters into reds and golds. We're sitting just outside the hotel we work at together. Well, that we *used* to work at together. Today was my last day. I'm going back to New York tomorrow morning. I have a conference and then I'm hoping to get a new job.

I'll miss these summer sunsets. There's something magical about the summer sun here. I've gotten used to the heat and the humidity. The food is different and the fruit is sweeter here. I love this place. I'll miss just about everything here on the islands.

"Something like that," I tell her. I set my plate in the sand off to the side and shrug.

"Okay. Now I know something's wrong. You're not eating *any* of the mango on your plate." She frowns at me, her big brown eyes concerned. She's only a couple years older than me, so we've become friends as well as co-workers. "Who died? Is your dad okay?"

"My dad's fine," I assure her. "He just had another scan and they didn't find anything."

The doctors found a cancerous polyp in my dad's intestine two years ago. There had been surgeries and medicines. I'd gone back to New York as much as I could during it all, and luckily the doctors don't see signs of any regrowth. I still worry about him, though.

"Well, that's good." Julie is still looking at me like I'm some sort of puzzle. "So what is it? Something is bothering you. You never pass up fresh mango. Are you worried about getting another job? You'll have one in no time."

Strangely, getting a new job isn't on the top of my list of worries right now. It should be, but it's not. I sigh. "Have you ever heard me mention Jonathan? The younger brother of the family my dad works for?"

"You mean Jonathan Lewis, son of billionaire James Lewis and heiress Deborah Lewis, brother of also billionaire business owner Christopher Lewis. Greek God Jonathan. God's gift to humanity? Perfection in human form? The most handsome, kind, smart, funny, and amazing man to have ever walked the planet?" Julie ticks his attributes off on her fingers before turning to face me. "You mean that Jonathan?"

"I guess I have mentioned him," I say, feeling a little embarrassed. Surely I wasn't that bad?

"Only a couple or seven hundred times," she says with a dismissive wave of her hand. "You lived in the same house as him, right?"

"Basically. My dad is a butler for the Lewis family. Part of his pay is that he gets an apartment over the storage area to live in. When we moved there, it was perfect for a widower and his young daughter. I grew up on the Lewis house grounds, but I wasn't exactly a preferred playmate. You know, being the butler's daughter and all."

"Don't dirty yourself with the help," Julie says, feigning a posh British accent. "I get it. Living close, but socially miles away."

I nod. "Exactly. I was always an outsider looking in at them."

"You're the little mermaid watching the prince," Julie says. She leans back, elbows in the sand and her eyes on the sunset. "What has your precious Jonathan done to get you so despondent you won't eat?"

"He's getting married." The words stick in my throat like I've swallowed too many pieces of taffy.

"I'm so sorry, Nora." Julie sits up a little and pats my shoulder, her face full of sympathy. "How'd you find out?"

"It was in the gossip column of the paper."

Julie sighs. "Why are you reading the gossip column? You don't live there. You don't need that."

"It's the only way I can find out what Jonathan is doing," I explain. "My father won't tell me anything and he's gotten the other household staff to stay quiet too."

"I can't imagine why," Julie says with an obvious eye roll. I stick my tongue out at her.

"It's just a harmless crush," I tell her. "I just want to know how he's doing."

"Right. Harmless." Julie shakes her head and sighs. "Okay. So the love of your life is getting married. I'm assuming it's not to you."

"Nope." I shake my head. "Despite the fact that we basically grew up in the same house, I'm not actually one-hundred percent certain he even knows my name."

Julie winces. "Ouch."

"Yeah." I sigh. I look out at the sunset and feel like everything in my world is falling apart. I know that's hyperbole, but it still feels hopeless. I'm used to seeing him with beautiful women on his arm, but he goes through relationships like regular people go through plastic cups: quickly and without any kind of actual permanence.

I never thought he'd ever actually find someone. I never thought that I'd have to face the fact that it wasn't me.

"You going to be okay?" Julie asks.

I point to my uneaten fruit. "What do you think?"

"Right. Not okay. Not even a little bit," Julie replies. "At least you're going home tomorrow. Maybe you can talk some sense into him."

I chuckle, but there's not much joy in it. "You have way too much faith in me. I get near him and I turn into this mumbling dolt. I'm suddenly thirteen years old and awkward as hell every time I talk to him. It's not pretty."

"Wow. You've got it bad for him," Julie says, shaking her head a little. She looks over at me. "Maybe you can stay here a little longer? I'm sure the boss would allow it."

"I don't have a job here anymore," I remind her. "They closed my position and hired a social media guru."

"It's not going to last," Julie tells me. "You had bookings up thirty percent."

"Yeah, and then I asked for a raise," I say with a shrug. "Apparently, what I do isn't worth paying me for."

"They're stupid," Julie assures me. "They're just used to getting it for practically free."

The hotel here did get a good deal on me.

Deborah, Jonathan's mother, got me this position a few

years ago, but I made it my own. I have a degree in business, and somehow that made Deborah think that I should work as a hospitality specialist at a very elite hotel in the Caribbean. She got me an internship and I tried it out.

Turns out, I have my father's skills in hospitality. Combined with the business sense I got from my mother, I am really good at running hotels.

I've worked here long enough for peanuts. I have the experience and skills now that I deserve more than the bare minimum. I've made this company hundreds of thousands of dollars, yet they won't give me a dollar raise.

So, I'm going to an industry conference in New York and getting myself a new job.

"I did consider staying," I tell Julie, looking around the beach. The island feels like home. "But I need to think of my career."

"So you're going home. You could get a job anywhere in the world, but you're going all the way back to New York."

"Yes. Because of my dad," I reply. "I know he's had clean scans, but I'm still worried about him. He's all alone. I want to be closer to him."

Julie gives me a look that says she doesn't entirely believe me. "Right. Jonathan didn't even factor in a little bit to the decision to go back to New York instead of literally anywhere else in the world."

"Fine. Jonathan is part of the reason." I sigh, knowing that she's right but not enjoying being called out on it. "But only a little bit."

"Your crush on him is not healthy," Julie tells me.

"Why do you think Deborah sent me to the Caribbean? Why do you think my dad practically pushed me out of the airplane to get here?" I pick up a handful of the pure white sand and play with it in my hands. "I know Jonathan's a dream. He's so far out of my league that we're playing different sports. He lives in a freaking castle and I'm just the butler's daughter. The feelings I have for him are all in my head. I know that."

"But?" Julie smiles gently at me, knowing that there's more.

"But I need to see him one last time," I tell her. "I'm more confident and sophisticated now. Maybe he'll see me as me, instead of the shy little girl that lives over the garage."

"You are the very definition of confidence and sophistication. And I'm only being a little sarcastic." She smiles at me and bumps me gently with her shoulder. "You know you'll always have a home here."

"I know, and thank you," I tell her. I give her a hug that she returns. Together, we look out at the nearly dark sky. It's almost time to leave this paradise.

"Did you like it here?" Julie asks.

"I love it here," I say honestly. "If it weren't for my dad, I would probably never leave."

"And Jonathan," Julie corrects.

"And Jonathan," I agree.

"You even blush when you say his name," Julie says with a laugh. She shakes her head. "What about the older brother? You always talk about Jonathan, but never the other one."

"Christopher?" I don't feel the same warmth I do when I say Jonathan's name.

"You don't like him?" Julie asks, shifting to a more comfortable position on the sand.

"He's fine," I say with a shrug. "I liked him more when we were little. He's always been serious, though. Even as a kid he had a hard time having fun. When his dad died, he just dove into being a businessman completely."

"You say that like it's a bad thing," Julie observes.

"It's not, it's just..." I stop and think for a second how to describe Christopher. "Where Jonathan is playful, Christopher is stern. Jonathan is loving, but Christopher has no heart. Jonathan is admittedly, a playboy. He's always falling in love. Christopher? I'm sure he's had dates, but... he's cold and calculating. Business is everything to him. He makes pre-ghost Ebeneezer Scrooge look like a freaking Santa Claus."

"Wow." Julie tilts her head, imagining what Christopher must be like.

"He works on Christmas," I continue. "He asked for a fax machine for his tenth birthday. I don't think the man even knows how to have fun. The only reason he knows how to smile is that it's a good business tactic."

"I can see why you want to be with the younger brother," Julie says. "Christopher sounds awful."

"It's not like I have a chance with either of them," I tell her. "I don't know if Christopher is even capable of love. His idea of a long term relationship is letting his date order dessert. And Jonathan..." My face falls and my chest tightens. "He's getting married. He finally found a love that sticks."

"You going to be okay?" Julie asks again, putting her arm around me.

"I'm probably going to pine away and never love again," I say dramatically. "I'll just hoard cats. It'll be fine."

Julie laughs, giving me a gentle hug with the arm around me. "I'm going to miss you."

"Same," I tell her. I look over at my fruit. I'm still not hungry. "You want my plate?"

"Sure," Julie says, taking it from me. "You should go home and pack."

I hand her the plate and then stand up. I make sure to move downwind of her before I dust the fine sand from my work uniform.

"You'll tell me how it goes with Jonathan?" Julie asks, popping a piece of mango into her mouth.

"Every time he so much as looks in my direction, I'll call you," I assure her. I give her a self-deprecating smile. "So, you'll hear from me around next Christmas."

I'm home.

I feel it in my bones as the cab rolls past the immense iron gates. I hope that maybe I'll catch a glimpse of Jonathan. Maybe he'll be out in the garden and I'll be able to pass innocently by and say hello.

It would be nice just to see him.

The house comes into view. It's practically a castle. There are two tennis courts, multiple swimming pools, gardens, gazebos, patios, tea gardens, a koi pond, and a solarium. The house has sixteen bedrooms, a matching number of bathrooms, and three kitchens. The wine cellar is bigger than most houses.

There's a good reason why this house needs a butler. The house is bigger and has more amenities than some hotels.

The cab drops me off in front of the main house rather than the tiny apartment above the storage area. It's not a far walk, so I don't protest. I can pretend to this one cab driver that I belong here. That I'm not broke and from a poor family. I pay him, giving a good tip. As far as this cab driver is concerned, I'm the billionaire heiress that owns this whole place.

Not just the butler's daughter.

Familiar scents and sounds fill my ears. I smell gardenias and roses in the garden mixed with the soft scent of warm summer trees. The buzz of lawn mowers is in the distance and everywhere I look, people are scurrying and hurrying around making sure the house is picture perfect.

Everything is exactly the way I left it. There's the garage with the apartment I grew up in perched above it. The house and the grounds. The neat paths of crushed gravel and the carefully manicured gardens and lawns.

This was the last place I saw Jonathan. He was, of course, with another girl. They were sitting under a tree having a picnic. She laughed at his jokes and he smiled at her. Neither one of them had seen me near the front door. I'd been invisible then, just the hired help.

He'd leaned over and kissed her, putting his hand in her hair as he tasted her.

I'd imagined that I was that girl so many times. I'd imagined what it would feel like to have Jonathan kiss me under a tree in the summer.

In my mind, it was always heaven. I sigh and begin the walk around the main house and to my father's small apartment.

That's when I see him.

Jonathan is out playing tennis. He's just as I remember him. Better even.

He's tall and trim as he effortless runs after the ball. He's got lush brown hair that styled in a carefree way that I know takes forever. I can't see them from here, but I know he has piercing blue eyes that make all the girls go weak in the knees.

He's laughing as he lobs the ball back to his companion. I consider walking over and saying hello, but I'm still in my traveling clothes and I have two suitcases with me. I haven't done my hair and I'm sure I'm a mess.

I sigh, and leave Jonathan behind yet again.

Tucked back behind the trees and out of sight is a building for storage. This is where they keep the lawn mowers and pool equipment. This is where spare tables and pavilions wait for the lavish dinner parties the Lewis family loves to throw. This is where they keep all the things that make the house look beautiful and the parties run smoothly. It's all out of sight. Just like my father, the butler. Integral, but unseen.

There's a set of wooden stairs with a rickety handrail leading up to the apartment. My father has replaced the rail three times, but it always seems to be loose no matter how many nails and screws he uses.

I run up the stairs and open the door to my childhood home.

My father is in the small kitchen, a frown on his face as he opens and closes drawers. He's still wearing his butler's uniform, but the jacket is unbuttoned and his tie is crooked. I can hear him mumbling about always losing his keys as he checks another drawer.

He looks older than when I saw him last, although, in my mind he'll always be the giant of a man that can do anything. In my head, he's the man he was when I was seven and could keep the monsters away just by growling into the closet.

There's more gray in his hair now and less hair in

general. He's thinner and more worn. His brown eyes are still warm and bright, but there are wrinkles around them that aren't in my childhood memories.

I came home from the Caribbean when the doctor's first found something two years ago. I'd nearly stayed, but Dad had insisted that I go back after the surgery. I'd called him everyday and had the other household staff giving me daily updates. He'd been fine, but it had been stressful.

We'd lost my mother when I was six. I didn't want to lose him too. I set my bags down by the door.

"Nora!" My father's eyes light up as he sees me in the doorway. The years fall away from him, and suddenly he looks like the man in my head again. "You're home!"

He hurries across the living room, dodging the small coffee table piled high with books. He wraps me up in a giant bear hug that makes me feel small and safe again. I close my eyes, breathing in the scents of silver polish and freshly washed linens.

"Hi, Dad." I'm home now.

"Let me look at you," he says, pulling back and holding me at arm's length. "You look more like your mother everyday, thank the lord. I like the way you have your hair. The lighter color suits you and I love the cut."

Yet again, my hand goes to my hair and smooths out the light blonde strands. "Julie made me get rid of the bangs," I tell him. "You like it?"

"I love it," he assures me with a smile. "It's much more you."

I grin at him. "Thanks, Dad."

"How did you get here?" he asks, pulling me back in for one more quick hug. "I was just coming to get you."

I bend over and pick his car keys up from a stack of

books and hand them to him. "I took a cab. I figured it was something with the family, especially since you didn't call."

My father refuses to answer his personal cell phone during working hours. When he is on duty, that is all he does. He takes his job very seriously.

I go to my bags, happy to have an excuse to talk about something other than Jonathan. While he might be my favorite subject, Jonathan is not my father's preferred conversation topic.

"I got you some things," I say, going to one of the bags. I unzip the zipper and dig around for a moment before I find what I'm looking for. "Here."

Dad laughs as I hand him the gifts I got for him this time. There's a bottle of good Caribbean rum, a sailing ship made from driftwood, and a pirate hat.

Dad puts the hat on his head and squints one eye. "Arrrgh, matey!"

I can't help but laugh. I love to see this silly side of him. It's a side so few get to see. As a butler, it's his job to be polite and perfect. There is no goofiness or playfulness when he's with the Family. With them, he's a paragon of polite subservience. With me, he's silly and playful.

I love my dad.

"These are lovely. Thank you." He kisses my cheek, making me smile. His eyes narrow. "You ready for your conference?"

I nod. "I'll go to the city tomorrow and hopefully come home with a new job."

I better. I'm not sure I can walk past Jonathan again without my heart breaking.

CHAPTER 3

The conference is packed to the point of being overwhelming. Every travel agent, hotel manager, social media guru, and everyone with an interest in becoming one is here with at least three others. I didn't expect it to be this crowded.

Suddenly, I'm a little more nervous about my job prospects. I'm really good at what I do, but it's still hard to stand out in a crowd like this. How am I supposed to wow a company when there's fifteen other people trying to do the same thing?

I attend a couple of sessions, and eat the conference luncheon, but I'm not really learning anything new. These classes are geared toward beginners, and I'm anything but that. There's only one more class for the day, but I can't really stomach the idea of sitting through another basic class on why having a social media presence is necessary, so I go out to the hotel lobby.

The big hotel foyer leads to a bar and a restaurant as well as a comfortable seating area. There's a fireplace, but it isn't turned on since it's summer. I see several people sitting with laptops and working. I wish I had brought my computer. I could at least be filling out job applications if I had. For as expensive as this conference was, I am losing hope of this being a success.

There is supposed to be a fancy cocktail party together tonight. I'm hoping that I'll meet some big names and make some connections. It's still an hour away, but I go to the bathroom and change now.

I brought my lucky little black dress. I found it in a secondhand store, but it's Gucci and it looks amazing on me. I pull back my hair and try to find a balance between sexy and professional. It's a difficult thing to accomplish in a hotel bathroom. When I think I have something that will work, I head back out to the lobby to wait for the cocktail party to start.

I get a glass of free complimentary water since it's all I can afford and sit down at an empty table near a big window. I sit and watch the busy city streets outside, trying to not regret my choice of coming here. It's just the first day of the conference. It has to get better, right?

"Excuse me, but is this seat taken?"

My eyes go wide and my heart starts to flutter. I know that voice.

There's no way it could actually be him.

I turn, fairly sure that I've fallen asleep and am now dreaming.

Standing with a cup of coffee in his hand is Jonathan Lewis.

Yup. Definitely dreaming, but I don't dare wake up.

"What?" My eyes bug out of my head a little bit as he grins at me.

"Can I sit here?" he asks, pointing to the empty seat across from me. "Everywhere else is full."

I glance around and realize the lobby is now packed. The bar is at least three deep to get drinks and conference attendees are spilling out of their sessions in waves. Every chair and couch is filled with bodies. Except the one chair sitting across from me.

This is the first time in my life that I'm fairly sure that the universe doesn't hate me.

"No, no. Please sit." I motion to him, feeling my cheeks heat. "You can always sit with me, Jonathan."

He pauses, his body stopping for a moment before settling into the chair. His smile is a little less sure, but still enough to make my stomach do happy flipflops that it's directed at me.

"You know me?" he asks.

"Of course I know you," I tell him. "I've known you forever."

"You have?" A quick, embarrassed smile flickers across his face. "Are you sure? I get people who think they've met me all the time."

This is when I realize that he doesn't recognize me. He doesn't remember me as the shy, quiet girl from long ago. He doesn't remember that I've visited for every Christmas, but then again, he probably didn't really see me. I don't think I've changed that much, but it's possible that I have.

"You're Jonathan Lewis. You like to play singles tennis better than doubles. You always put extra whip cream in your cocoa. You like to wear blue because you know it brings out your eyes. Your favorite car is the blue Porsche you got when you were sixteen."

There's a lot more, but that seems like enough.

He shakes his head. "The Porsche isn't my favorite," he corrects me. "Everyone knows it's the red McLaren."

I shake my head. "Nope, it's the blue Porsche. The red McLaren was a gift from your mother and you only drive it to make her happy. You love that blue car."

He narrows his beautiful blue eyes at me and takes a sip of coffee. "You either know me very well, or you are a very good stalker."

It's concerning to me that I'm probably a little bit of both.

"How are things going for you?" I ask. A big stupid smile fills my face as I stare at him. I've kept up with all the gossip magazines, but it's better to hear it from the source. I want to hear him tell me that he's doing well.

"I'm good. You?" He sits like he owns the place. His broad shoulders are relaxed and there's a hint of a smile on his face. There's not an ounce of being uncomfortable that he doesn't know who I am.

Me on the other hand, I'm a wreck. My heart is pounding. I'm sweating, and I think I might puke from happiness. Jonathan Lewis is talking to me. Actually, really, not in my imagination, talking to me.

"I'm great," I gush. *Reign it in, Nora.* I tell myself. *You are calm and sophisticated. Act like it.* "What are you doing here?"

"I'm meeting a friend for dinner across the street," he replies. "But they're running late and the restaurant is somehow even more crowded than this place."

We both look around at the lobby full of people.

"And, the coffee cart here has the best coffee in the entire city," he tells me. "I'd rather wait in here."

I can see the coffee cart. The barista is a pretty blonde that looks like just his type.

"Well, you are certainly welcome to share my table," I tell him. "I'm definitely happy for the company."

He grins at me.

This is my opportunity. This is my chance. We can finally have a real conversation. I can have him fall head over heels in love with me. Maybe we'll make-out at Lover's Lane. Maybe he'll pull into the garage and close the door so that no one can see us. Maybe we'll get married and live happily ever after.

And I'm getting so far ahead of myself it's ridiculous.

Calm and sophisticated, I remind myself. He's barely been sitting at the table for thirty seconds and doesn't know who I am.

"I appreciate that," he replies, flashing me another smile. "Though, I'd love to know your name. Just to help jog my memory."

I nearly tell him. But, for the first time in years, I feel like I have a chance catching Jonathan's attention. I have a real chance.

"You're going to have to figure it out on your own," I reply. "I'm sure it will come to you."

"Oh, I'm sure it will." His eyes go up and down my body, and I heat from head to toe. He just checked me out.

I feel like I'm going to pass out. My heart is going out of control and I'm suddenly really glad I haven't eaten anything yet. I'm sure he'd remember me forever if I threw up on him.

"So, why are you here?" Jonathan asks.

"I'm here for the conference," I reply, pointing to my conference lanyard and badge.

"You must be presenting," he says. "You look like you must be good at your job. Which is?"

"Nice try. I'm not giving you more info so you can figure me out." I laugh, feeling the butterflies in my stomach dance. "But I'm not presenting. I'm just an attendee. "

He leans over, looking at my conference badge. I'm suddenly very aware of the cut on my dress and that Jonathan Lewis is checking me out. The Universe was kind enough to put me in my best dress for this. It's definitely fate that he's here talking to me. Jonathan's eyes go up and down my body, and I heat from head to toe. I don't miss the slight dilation in his pupils when he looks back up at me.

"The Traveling Destination: a conference for all things traveling," he reads off my badge. "It sounds very interesting. Could I see your badge?"

"Nope," I reply, quickly tucking it away. Luckily my name is on the side facing me. It is pure luck that he didn't just read my name off my badge. "You aren't going to figure it out that easily."

"Smart and beautiful," he muses, taking a sip of his coffee. "Now I really am going to have to figure you out."

I giggle with nerves. He's clueless, and somehow that makes me hopeful. The butler's daughter never had a chance with Jonathan, but maybe the suave and charming woman in the hotel lobby does.

"How is your mother?" I ask, changing the subject. "I haven't seen her since I got back."

"Since you got back?" he repeats, ignoring my question. "That means you've been away. That would explain a travel conference. Who do I know that's been traveling? "

I just smile, but my heart skips a beat. What if he figures me out? I don't want him to realize that I'm just the boring daughter of a man that works for him. I don't want to have him ignore me the way he has for most of my life. He sees me now.

"Are you a friend of Becky Sinclair? She's traveling the world for Instagram," he says.

"No. That's not how you know me." I grin at him. "I'll give you a hint. You've known me from before I started traveling."

"That doesn't really help," he tells me. He looks me over again and sighs. "There is something so familiar about you. I just can't figure it out." He pales a little. "We aren't related, are we?"

"Oh, god, no." I vehemently shake my head. "Not even a little bit."

He lets out a breath. "Good. I can only imagine if I brought home a cousin."

I blink twice. He is thinking of bringing me home? Something heats in the pit of my stomach and curls around my spine. I like the idea of him bringing me home very much.

"Well, just know that I'm an old friend, then," I reply with a smile. "Definitely not a relative."

"You really aren't going to tell me?" he asks, putting on big puppy-dog eyes.

For the first time ever, I'm not a stammering mess around Jonathan. I'm being flirtatious and clever. It helps that he has no idea who I am, so I have the advantage. He doesn't recognize me, so I can be anyone at all.

And right now, I am going to be awesome.

"Come back tomorrow, and I'll tell you who I am," I say. "If you haven't figured it out by then."

"You're going to make me wait until tomorrow?" His eyes go wide. "What if you try and disappear?"

He doesn't usually have to work this hard for a girl. Usually, they are falling all over him like I want to do.

"I won't disappear. I'll be at this conference for the next two days," I tell him. "But I'm staying close to where you live. I have family in the area."

If that isn't the understatement of the year, I'm not sure what is.

"Beautiful and mysterious. I can't wait to find out more about you," he tells me. He reaches out and takes my hand in his.

Today might be the best day of my life.

"What if I asked you to lunch?" He flashes me a grin. "I'm sure my friend won't mind having a beautiful lady join us."

Somehow the best day of my life just got better.

"And you're hoping that he'll recognize me," I add.

Jonathan just grins. "Maybe."

I chew on my lip for a moment. Am I ready for this? I know I shouldn't skip the conference cocktail party, but the opportunity of spending time with Jonathan is too tempting, no matter how much I paid for his conference. It's just a cocktail party. I feel a little guilty, but not enough to stop.

"I'd love to," I tell him.

"Come with me." He gracefully rises from his chair and holds out his hand. "It'll be my treat."

I'm pretty sure I've died and gone to heaven.

CHAPTER 4

I'm on cloud nine. If there were a cloud ten or eleven, I'd be on cloud fifteen.

I'm going out on a date with Jonathan Lewis. The man I have loved since boys stopped having cooties.

I'm positively giddy.

He holds my hand as we walk out of the hotel lobby and across the street. My heels click on the sidewalk as we walk through the twilight. I see people look over at us and smile. I hope that they see two people who are meant to be together.

The restaurant is way out of my price range. Most nice restaurants in the city are. Once again, I'm sure this is fate. The universe is setting me up for something amazing. Why else would I be wearing my best dress? Why else would Jonathan happen to be having dinner in the restaurant across from my conference.

It's fate. It has to be.

Jonathan goes to the check in desk and gives his name. The lobby for the restaurant is still packed with people, but the waitress simply waves Jonathan and me inside. I try to ignore the angry glares directed my way as we pass those that are waiting.

I've been waiting my whole life, I think to myself. *It's my turn.*

Jonathan pulls out my chair for me like a gentleman. I smile and sit carefully, making sure the hem of my skirt doesn't ride up too much. I can't help but notice that Jonathan looks at my legs. I like the way his face goes a little bit hungry for a split second before he goes to his own seat. We sit with only a corner of the table between us. A candle flickers romantically.

"Would you like some wine?" Jonathan asks, motioning to a waitress. I nod. A little courage juice might help stop the excited shaking in my fingers. He orders two glasses of white wine for us.

"Where's your friend?" I ask, looking around. There's two empty seats at our table.

"He'll be here in a minute," Jonathan replies, checking his phone. "Now, tell me all about yourself."

I laugh, seeing through the ruse easily.

"Let's see, what can I tell you that doesn't give my identity away," I say, tapping my lower lip with my finger while I think. "I was recently in the Caribbean."

"I love the Caribbean," Jonathan tells me. "I found the best little resort there. Maybe I can take you some time. It's amazing."

The idea of a Caribbean adventure with Jonathan makes my brain go all woozy as blood rushes to other parts of my body.

"I think I'd like that." The words come out in a whispery moan that makes Jonathan smile and me blush.

"What else?" Jonathan asks. "I have to know more about you."

"What do you want to know?" I'll tell him anything. Everything.

Jonathan's eyes go to mine and I'm lost in them. He scoots his chair just a little bit closer to me, our legs touching under the table. I feel like he could lean over and kiss me at any moment. I close my eyes, letting fate take control.

"Jonathan!" A man in a suit greets him, ruining my moment. I'm guessing this is the friend Jonathan is meeting. I wish he hadn't interrupted, especially when Jonathan pulls away from me to shake the man's hand.

"Is this your soon-to-be lovely bride? I haven't met her yet," the man asks, smiling brightly at me. I flush hard.

"No, this is my very good friend, um..." Jonathan says, trailing off. He starts casually, like he's not being called out for being with another woman, but gets nervous when he realizes he still doesn't know my name.

"Nora," I said, extending my hand to the newcomer.

"Oh, I just thought..." The man glances back and forth between the two of us and then clears his throat. "It's very nice to meet you."

"Likewise." I try to copy Jonathan's easy manner, but I'm embarrassed. My father would be appalled. I hope that I sound as confident as the women Jonathan usually dates. Most of them are models or famous actresses.

The only upside is that there is no way Jonathan's friend is going to reveal who I am.

"I hate to do this to you, Jonathan, but I can't stay," the man says. "My brother is in the hospital. Apparently he sat on a wine glass or something."

"That sounds terrible," Jonathan says. "And very painful."

The man nods. "Anyway, I'm on my way to the hospital now. I'm sorry about dinner. Maybe Christopher can join you or something."

"Christopher is working. He's always working," Jonathan says, voicing my thoughts. He shrugs. "It's okay. I invited *Nora* to join us," he says, letting me know that he knows my name now. "So I'm not alone."

The man turns and looks at me. "I'm sorry about all this."

"Another time," I tell him with a smile. "I hope your brother is okay."

"Me too. It's nice to meet you. Sorry again, Jonathan." The man smiles and then disappears out of the restaurant.

"Sat on a wine glass. That sounds awful," I say, being just a little more careful with the wine glass full of water on the table.

"No kidding." Jonathan makes a pained grimace, but then shifts it into a smile. "But it works out for me. Now I have you all to myself."

I giggle, feeling love struck and excited.

"Have you ever been here before?" Jonathan asks.

I shake my head. "No. This is a new restaurant to me."

"Me too," he replies. "We shall explore it together."

The love struck feeling intensifies and I'm afraid I might melt into happy goo.

The waitress comes with the wine and takes our order. I get the risotto and Jonathan orders a scallop dish.

"So, my mysterious date likes risotto," Jonathan observes when the waitress leaves us. He grins at me. "Not only beautiful, but you have good taste too."

I try not to gulp at my wine.

The man of my dreams thinks I'm beautiful and mysterious. We are talking. Flirting. We're both happy. I wish this could be how I feel every time I see him. I wish this was the start of our life together. That this would be our meet-cute that we tell our children. But he is supposedly getting married.

The future I have planned for us is all just in my head. As usual.

Still, I need to know for sure.

I clear my throat. "I heard that you're getting married."

His answer comes fast as he pulls his hand away. "No, no. I'm not." He chuckles nervously.

"You're not?" Hope starts to rise in my chest. I try not to let it fill my lungs and overpower me, but it's hard. He's not engaged. The dream of the two of us could still happen. "You're really not engaged?"

"No, not engaged." He clears his throat. "I am kind of seeing someone. It's not serious though."

"Oh." I'm not sure how to feel about that, but I'm still just relieved he's not engaged.

"We're not exclusive or anything," Jonathan assures me, tossing a smile my way. "It's based on business. My brother wants to merge his business with hers. He's doing it through me." He pauses and then laughs. "It sounds dirty when I say it like that."

I laugh, feeling my fears start to vanish. He's not engaged. The only reason he's dating someone is for business. There's a chance that the stars are aligning for us to be together.

"So your brother wants you to date her?" I ask.

"Yeah. It's all part of his business plan," he replies.

"But I'm thinking I need to find my own way. My brother isn't always right about everything."

I raise my eyebrows.

"Don't worry about that, though," Jonathan tells me. "I'm more interested in finding out more about you. Do you like to play tennis?"

"I'm actually pretty terrible at tennis," I admit. "I'm more of a swimmer."

"That's too bad," Jonathan replies. "I'm not much of a swimmer. That's more my brother's sport."

"Maybe I haven't found the right person to play with," I tell him, not wanting him to lose interest with any part of me.

His eyes glow in the candlelight as he grins at me. "I'm always looking for someone to play tennis with me."

Dinner is a dream come true.

Jonathan is everything I knew he was going to be. He's smart and funny. He's charming and incredibly handsome. He asks me questions, really trying to get to know me. Granted, I know that he's just trying to figure me out, but I don't really care.

I'm ready to marry him right now, to be honest.

"Do you work with my brother?" Jonathan asks as he finishes his meal. Our knees touch under the table and every time he moves, my heart speeds up just a little.

I scrunch up my face and shake my head. "No."

"My mother?" He watches me carefully, seeing how I react. "You don't look like one of her DAR ladies, but they are trying to recruit younger ladies these days."

"I have no involvement in DAR." *I doubt they'd let me in the door.* "I don't work with your mother, although she is a very nice lady."

He frowns, studying my face. "I'm going to figure this out."

"I'm sure you will," I tell him, patting at my lips with a napkin. "Or you'll just find out tomorrow."

"Tomorrow feels like it's forever," he tells me. "A whole dinner and all I know is that you don't play tennis, you like to swim, you don't work with my family, and you were in the Caribbean recently."

I just grin at him. "You also learned that I'm allergic to penicillin and I still have my appendix."

"Yes, because that helps me so much." He rolls his eyes making me laugh.

He leans over and touches my hand. I feel like this is a real date. He's smiling at me and touching me at every opportunity. This is how people fall in love. This is how love stories go.

Jonathan pays without even looking at the bill.

"Thank you for a wonderful dinner," I say as we leave the restaurant. The night is cool and I wish I had brought a sweater. I wrap my arms around me. I'm not used to the weather here yet. It feels cold to me after the heat of the Caribbean islands.

"Thank you for being such wonderful company," he replies.

"Can I interest you in a drink?" I ask him. I'm hoping it will lead to more. That all my dreams will come true.

Jonathan starts to nod, a sexy as hell grin crossing his face. He steps closer to me, his body pressing into mine for a moment, teasing me with what could happen next.

And then his pocket vibrates.

"Excuse me for a second," he says, pulling out his phone. He looks at the number and frowns. "Hey, Christopher. What's wrong now?"

I can hear Christopher's voice on the other end, but not what he's saying. He doesn't sound happy.

"I'm just having dinner," Jonathan tells him. "No need to get riled about it. Are you having me watched?"

Jonathan puts his hand over the speaker and rolls his eyes.

"Yes, it was with a woman, but I am still allowed to eat, aren't I? I'm not doing anything wrong."

I think I hear Christopher say something about Adeline in response, but I'm not sure. Adeline is the name of the woman I thought Jonathan was engaged to marry. But Jonathan said he was just dating Adeline Timbers, founder of the TimberTech company. He's certainly allowed to date more than one person at a time. He gives one word answers to Christopher, growing more agitated with every sentence.

Something about the conversation makes my stomach tighten uncomfortably and my shoulders tense. There's something here that I'm missing, but I'm not sure what it is. Surely Jonathan wouldn't lie to me about his engagement, would he?

"Of course I'll come to the office," Jonathan says with a sigh. Christopher says something that makes him roll his eyes. "Yes, I'll do it right now."

He clicks off the phone and stuffs it into his pocket.

"Trouble?" I ask.

"Just my brother being obnoxiously nosy and controlling." Irritation thrums through Jonathan's voice. "I'm really sorry, but I'm going to have to pass on the drink."

I have no concrete reason, but I blame Christopher for my evening being cut short. Granted, Jonathan hadn't actually said yes yet, but he looked like he was going to. The fact that I heard Adeline's name in their phone conversation makes me even more suspicious about why Christopher is calling Jonathan into the office.

"But I'll be back here tomorrow," Jonathan promises. He reaches for my hands, taking them in his as he gazes into my eyes. All thoughts of Christopher leave my head, especially when Jonathan brings my hands to his lips and kisses them. "Can I walk you home?"

He glances across the street to the hotel. I don't correct him that I'm not staying at the hotel with the conference. I'm not about to tell him where I really live.

"I'd like that."

He keeps hold of one of my hands, and together we cross the street. At the doorway to the hotel, he lets go, much to my sorrow.

"I'll see you tomorrow, Mystery Woman." The small smile and the sparkle in his eyes make the low tones of his voice even more sexy. "See you at ten."

I step forward, hoping for a goodnight kiss, but he pulls away. In moments, he lost to the crowds on the street.

I stare after him, aching for more yet amazed at what I got.

I had dinner with Jonathan Lewis. And tomorrow, I'll get even more.

CHAPTER 5

I get to the hotel extra early the next morning, taking the first train into the city. I don't want Jonathan to see me leaving, so I make sure to leave well before he is even awake. I am excited about this surprise.

I'm not sure how Jonathan is going to react when I tell him who I am. I hope he doesn't lose all interest in me once he finds out who I am. We had such a connection yesterday that I can't imagine that he'd be anything but excited. He's dated people not in his social sphere before.

Still, I'm nervous. I barely slept last night and the few hours I did sleep were filled with wonderful dreams of Jonathan. For once, my dreams actually had some substance and weren't completely made up of conversations I'd wished we'd have.

He isn't coming until the end of the day. I wish I had his phone number so I could tell him to come earlier. I hate waiting.

The conference does nothing to help me pass the time

time. I'm too distracted to focus on the classes. I make a couple of contacts, but I still have no real job prospects.

I go to the lobby a good two hours early before it becomes crowded.

I sit down at the table, making sure I have the right seat in the right spot. I even splurge on a decaf coffee so that I have a real excuse to sit here. I don't want them to kick me out for a paying customer. I don't want anything to go wrong with this moment.

I've played this encounter out in my mind all day. I've come up with every possible scenario and while I wait, I play my favorite one in my head like I'm watching a movie.

He'll walk into the lobby, his hair catching the morning sunshine. He'll see me and smile. Those blue eyes will twinkle with delight as he walks toward me. He'll slide into his seat.

"Tell me who you are," he'll say, blue eyes focused only on me.

"It's me. Nora."

His eyes will widen and then he'll smile. "Nora? The butler's daughter?"

I'll nod, feeling nervous.

"I have loved you all along," he'll whisper. "I never thought I had a chance with you."

And then he'll kiss me.

Sure. That's how it's going to go.

I fiddle with my coffee, counting down the hours and

then the minutes until Jonathan arrives. Ten minutes before he's supposed to arrive, I am a mess of nerves. I wish I could get up and pace, but I'm afraid I might lose my spot. The lobby isn't crowded, but there aren't a lot of empty seats either. I am not going to do anything that might screw this up.

I stare at the door. Waiting. The sunlight is just bright enough that it makes it hard to see.

The front door slowly opens and I freeze. A man in a dark suit steps inside, his face still hidden in the shadows of the door. The evening light obscures his features. My heart thrills for a moment. He's the right height, the right build. He has dark hair.

I swallow hard as the man steps out of the shadows and into the lobby.

But it's not Jonathan. It's Christopher.

What in the world is Christopher doing here? Why would he be here, at this hotel? I stare at him as he looks around. His face is hard and his eyes angry as he searches the bar, the restaurant and then finally settle on me.

His eyes go wide for a moment and then the calm, calculating mask of a businessman he always wears goes right back on. He walks casually over to me, but there's a fierce determination that radiates off of him with every step.

"You." He glares at me. "It has to be you."

"C-Christopher?" I stumble on his name, not quite believing my eyes. I'm not sure what's going on.

"Tell me you're not meeting my brother here, Nora," Christopher says. "Tell me that it isn't you. Please tell me that it's a total coincidence that you're here."

I'm not surprised that Christopher recognizes me.

Nothing seems to get past him. He always remembers me when I come home for the holidays. He always sends a nice birthday card in the mail. He does that for all his employees and even though I'm not technically employed by him, he's shown me the same courtesy.

I shift in my seat. "I can't."

Christopher sighs. He closes his eyes and I'm sure he's counting to ten to keep his temper in control. It's more emotion than I usually see out of him. Once, I saw someone hit his car and ding the paint. He was cold fury, but in complete control.

He opens his eyes, focusing his blue gaze on me. There's disappointment and frustration there. "Can I take this seat?"

The words are so similar to what Jonathan asked me yesterday, yet so different at the same time. It's strange how the two men can look so alike and yet be so very different.

I nod. It's not like I can exactly say no.

"Why are you here, Christopher?" I ask. There's a cold feeling in the pit of my stomach. An anxious ache that isn't excited or happy.

"Yesterday I was in the middle of negotiation talks with TimberTech when I get a phone call that my brother is having a romantic dinner with someone who isn't his fiancee." Christopher sits tall in the chair. He doesn't sprawl into it like Jonathan did. Christopher is controlled and elegant.

"Having dinner with someone isn't a crime," I reply, crossing my arms.

"You're right," Christopher agrees. "But, imagine my concern when my brother comes into my office and starts telling me that he's met someone. A beautiful girl who says she knows him. Someone that's funny and sweet and sexy as hell. A mystery woman that has him seriously considering not getting married."

I try not to react to the idea that Jonathan thought me sexy as hell. Now is not an appropriate time for goofy smiles and giddy reactions.

"Where's Jonathan?" I ask quietly.

"He's still coming. He's just running a little bit late," Christopher replies. "I wanted to get here before he did and see this mystery woman for myself. I didn't expect to find you."

I swallow hard.

"He said he wasn't engaged," I say bluntly. "So is he?" I don't want to be the other woman, not even for Jonathan.

Christopher sighs and puts his hands on the table. "No, he's not technically engaged. But he does have a ring. And he has asked her father for permission. He just hasn't asked her yet."

I sink into my chair, this news hitting me like a punch to the gut.

"I think he has a fear of commitment," Christopher continues. "He keeps pushing it off. He keeps finding excuses and looking for reasons to back out."

"So he lied to me." I stare at Christopher's hands on the table. They are beautiful hands with long fingers and carefully trimmed nails. I'm waiting for the tears, but they haven't come yet. Perhaps I'm still just in too much shock. Maybe it's just the public setting.

"Technically, no. He's not engaged."

I look up at Christopher. "But he really is," I say. "He

has someone who loves him. Someone that isn't me. He didn't tell me he was taken."

"Can you blame him?" Christopher shakes his head. "The man who can barely commit to wearing the same shirt an entire day met a beautiful, funny woman with a mystery identity. A woman that obviously is attracted to him. I can't say I blame him. I'm not sure anyone could pass something like that up."

I frown raising my chin. "What do you mean by that? Obviously attracted?"

"Everyone but Jonathan knows how you feel about him," Christopher informs me. I feel like an idiot. A fool that everyone laughs at when I'm not around.

I close my eyes, wishing that this really was a dream and that I could just wake up. It's almost worse that it's real. At least if it were a dream, I wouldn't have to deal with Christopher or the growing knot of shame in my chest.

"Does he love her?" I ask him. I play with my empty coffee cup, watching it rather than Christopher.

"I think so. As much as my brother can love anyone," he replies. His voice is gentle and carries no judgment. "She's a good match for him, both mentally and financially. I honestly believe that he's just scared of finding something good for him. He is afraid of being happy."

Which means I'm not good for him. Or at least Christopher doesn't think I'm good for Jonathan. The dream I have of Jonathan loving me the way I love him is shattering. I've held onto it for years and today, I thought it might come true. There was a chance, but that chance was a lie.

I'm the escape plan. I'm Plan B. He doesn't want me. He just wants a way out.

"So what happens now?" I ask.

"First, you'll tell my brother who you are." Christopher sighs. "Then, you leave him alone. He isn't right for you."

His words hit me like bricks. "You don't know that."

Christopher sighs. "I'll make this easier. If you tell my brother that you aren't interested, that you had a great time but you were just messing with him, I will write you a check."

Anger flares up inside of me. "You can't buy me."

"Don't think of it that way," he says. Christopher's blue eyes are watching me, shrewd and businesslike. He's done so many deals and bargains, he could do this in his sleep. "Think of it as an investment in your future."

"And falling in love isn't an investment in the future?"

"He's not in love with you, Nora," he says gently, but the words still cut like a knife. "He's in love with the novelty of you."

"You don't know that." Anger heats my voice and I'm sure there are two bright red spots on my cheeks.

"This is just a business opportunity, Nora. Nothing personal," Christopher assures me. "Adeline is the owner of TimberTech. She is also the one pushing for a merger. If Jonathan breaks her heart, she'll pull out of everything. It would cost billions."

"Are you sure?

He shrugs like this should be obvious.

"If there wasn't billions of dollars on the line, would you still want me to leave him alone?" I ask.

I look up at Christopher, expecting to see him with cold eyes. Instead, he smiles sadly and shakes his head.

"No. You're wonderful, Nora. I think you could make anyone, even Jonathan, happy," he explains. "I know you've had a thing for Jonathan since you were kids. If it weren't for this deal, I wouldn't stand in your way. Like I said, this is just business."

I nod. "It's always business with you, isn't it?"

"That's what I'm told." Christopher shrugs. "So, what's it going to be, Nora?"

"I don't know," I say softly. I go over the options in my mind. We haven't settled on a number yet, but I'm sure it would be substantial. Christopher has never been cheap.

On the other hand, this is the love of my life.

"I won't take money," I tell Christopher. I'm not sure what I'm doing, but taking the money feels wrong. It feels cheap and tawdry. I need time to process this. I need time to learn more about just how close Jonathan is to marrying Adeline.

I won't break up a real relationship, but I won't give up Jonathan for no reason either.

Christopher's face hardens. He opens his mouth to give me a counter offer, but a shadow falls across the table.

"Christopher? What are you doing here?"

I didn't even see Jonathan walk up. Given the startled look on Christopher's face, neither did he. We both stare up at him, confusion on all our faces.

"Jonathan." Christopher rises from the chair, regaining his composure first. "I was just saying hello to Nora. You remember Nora. She's the daughter of our butler."

Jonathan frowns at his brother and then looks to me. He stares at me for a moment, his eyes growing wider with every second as recognition fills his face.

"Nora?" Jonathan says my name like he doesn't understand it. "*That* Nora?"

Jonathan's not looking at me like the strong, confident,

sexy woman he expected to see. I'm suddenly the thirteen year old girl with braces and frizzy hair. My heart starts pounding and the world threatens to spin out of control.

"Yes, it's Nora. I'm sure you remember her. She used to sneak into our pool sometimes." Christopher says nonchalantly.

"That's how you knew all that stuff about me," Jonathan whispers. He looks me up and down. "How did I not recognize you?"

"Her hair's lighter. I imagine it has to do with being out in the tropical sun," Christopher replies. He's not looking at his brother. He's looking at me. It's like he's trying to talk to me telepathically. I know that he wants me to do what he wants. *End it with him*, he's telling me.

I'm just not sure I'm ready to do it.

Jonathan is staring at me like I'm some long lost person back from the dead.

"Nora." Jonathan says my name again, shaking his head.

"Surprise." I give him a weak grin. I feel like I might throw up or pass out at any moment. There's suddenly not enough air around me.

Jonathan looks over at his brother. "Do you think we could get a moment alone? I'd like to talk to Nora."

"No, I don't think I can do that." Christopher shakes his head. "Not a chance."

The two of them glare at one another like two mountain goats about to butt heads over a female. They're having their own telepathic conversation. Sparks fly between them and I'm half afraid they're going to come to blows.

"I should go," I say, rising to my feet. I need to get out

of here. I need to get away from this and figure out what I should do.

"No, Nora, don't go," Jonathan says reaching for me. His hand rests gently on my arm, sending goosebumps of desire up my spine.

The goosebumps disappear when I look over at Christopher. His glare should be turning me to stone.

"No, I really should." I pull away, turning and walking away from the two of them, my heart pounding and my head reeling.

I hear my name called, but I don't look back.

I need time to process, and having the two of them staring at me and needing answers wasn't helpful. Jonathan is closer to marrying someone else then he let on.

I need space to think. My last few steps from the hotel come in at a near run. The hotel front desk staff glares at me as I sprint the last few meters out the door.

This wasn't how I had planned this to go.

CHAPTER 6

"Did you have a nice time at the conference yesterday?" Dad asks.

He comes and joins me at the small kitchen table, coffee cup in hand. He's almost ready for work, his suit pressed and perfect. There are no wrinkles on his pants and his vest and jacket hang neatly from a hanger by the door. They're perfectly pressed, too.

"The conference was fine," I tell him. It's not a total lie. The conference itself wasn't bad.

"You sure? You look exhausted this morning." Dad raises one eyebrow, the coffee mug halfway to his mouth. He has the paper in the other hand.

"I've just got a lot on my mind," I reply. I spent most of the night tossing and turning, thinking about Jonathan and Christopher. I still don't know what I want to do. I don't know what the right thing to do it.

"Okay. Well, I'm off to work. Apparently there's been some sort of incident today. It's going to be a busy day." Dad loses the stern look and smiles at me. He gets up and rinses his mug in the sink before putting it in the dish-washer. He comes around behind me and kisses the top of my head. "Don't get into too much trouble today, okay? I'm going to have my hands full as it is."

I roll my eyes, but smile. I watch as he goes to the door and carefully puts on his vest and jacket. He wears three-piece suits to serve the Family every day. His closet is full of dark blue, three-piece suits and no other cloth-ing. In fact, it's hard to think of my dad wearing anything else.

I set my coffee mug down on the table and stand up. I go to my father and help him tie his traditional tie. Today it's light blue. The ties are always solid colors or some-times demure patterns, but they are the only expression of himself my father ever wears. The light blue tie means he's happy today.

He smiles at me as I adjust the knot. My mother used to do this for him every morning. She's been gone a long time, but I still feel like I'm getting a special privilege when I get to do her job. The tie is an act of love, and I'm honored to do it.

Dad gives me a kiss on the cheek before opening the door. We both shout in surprise to see Christopher standing on our front porch, hand raised in mid-knock.

The change in my father from parental figure to butler is almost a physical transformation.

"Mr. Lewis, how can I help you?" My father doesn't sound surprised. When he's in work-mode, he never sounds surprised or angry or sad. He always sounds polite, calm, and capable, just as a butler should always sound.

Christopher's hand still hovers in the air mid-knock. His mouth opens slightly in shock.

"Um..." Christopher glances between my father and me. "I'm actually here to see Nora."

Dad turns his head to look at me, one eyebrow raised. In dad-butler mode, he might as well have his jaw hit the floor and shouted "WHAT?"

"I've got this, Dad," I tell my father, taking his place at the door. "You can go to work."

My dad looks back and forth between Christopher and me. Then he just sighs and shakes his head. Christopher moves to the side and my dad goes down the stairs.

I stand in the doorway, listening to my father's steps creak down the wooden stairs. Christopher finally lowers his hand, and now he wears a polite smile. I'm surprised he's not in a full business suit. He's actually wearing tan slacks and what appears to be a polo. I've never seen him look so informal on a work day. Granted, the shirt does have the LL Corp logo, but it's an incredibly casual thing for Christopher to be wearing. He's much like my father in that regard.

"You wanted to see me?" I ask Christopher. "If this is about last night..."

"No, no," he quickly cuts me off. "It's about business, actually."

Now I'm the one surprised. The idea that there is any business that Christopher would need from me is strange. He works primarily with telecommunications. I work in hotels, and while there is a TV in most hotels, that tends to be where the similarities of our jobs end.

"I have an opportunity to purchase a small, very exclusive resort," Christopher explains. "I need an insider to tell me if it's as good an investment as I think it is."

I raise one eyebrow. On the surface, it sounds plausible, but what are the odds that he just happened to have this kind of opportunity show up right now? What are the odds that a hotel offer would come up on Christopher Lewis's radar the day that he needs to distract a girl who is good with hotels.

Vegas wouldn't even have those odds.

I'm being managed. Christopher wants to keep me away from Jonathan and he's found something that I can't resist. He is making sure that I don't interfere with Jonathan by giving me a nice distraction.

"Why don't you hire someone?" I ask with an innocent shrug. "Why me?"

"I figured you're an expert," he explains. "I could hire someone, but I have you here. Now. Why waste time?"

Christopher looks calm except for the fact that he's playing with the cuticles on his right thumb. He used to do that during our dance lessons. It's his nervous tell. If I ever play poker with him, I'll win every hand.

"I don't know." I shake my head and frown.

"This sale is only available for a short time. There are other investors looking at it. I have a small window of opportunity on this."

"I don't know, Christopher..."

"I'll sweeten the deal," Christopher replies. "You do this for me, I'll put your name on the management transition team. It'll look good on any resume."

Christopher knows exactly how to get me. I chew on the inside of my cheek. I'm very clearly being "taken care of" and Christopher is making sure that I am no where near Jonathan. I don't like it, but the offer is a good one. The jobs I could get with that on my resume would be amazing. Something like this could be huge for my career.

This would give me the edge I need. This would be the key to getting a new job and the life I want.

Christopher smiles at me, knowing my internal discussion. Jonathan or my career? Which one will I pick?

"You can see Jonathan before we go and as soon as we get back," Christopher reminds me. "It's not like you'll never see him again."

I sigh. Christopher is right. Jonathan will still be here tomorrow, but this opportunity won't be. When opportunity knocks, it's important to answer the door. Besides, if Jonathan really is the love of my life, one day apart won't make a difference. It certainly hasn't mattered the past ten years.

"Okay. I'll do it." I sigh, but I think it's the right decision. "Do I need a business suit? Swimsuit?"

"Bring a swimsuit." He smiles at me and I almost believe it's real smile and not a business facsimile of one. He's probably just happy that his plan to keep me away from Jonathan is working.

"Okay. But first, I want to see Jonathan."

Christopher's smile fades back into one of polite business. The light leaves his eyes just a little bit. "That might be a little difficult. He's not really available."

"He's not?" I cross my arms, not really believing him.

"He's with our mother," Christopher replies. "She's at the hospital right now."

My eyes go wide. When my father said there was an incident at the house today, a hospital visit is not what I was expecting. I was thinking more along the lines of they'd run out of champagne or Mrs. Lewis was hosting a surprise party. Not that the matriarch of the family was seriously ill or injured. "What happened?"

"Oh, my mother's fine," Christopher quickly reassures me. "It's one of her friends. They're worried about her heart. Jonathan is close with the family as well, so he went with her."

"Oh. I'm sorry to hear that," I say, my hand going to my heart. "I'm glad your mom's okay, though."

Christopher nods. "You are welcome to call Jonathan. I'm sure he wants to talk to you. You can use my phone if you want. He won't pick up a strange number."

I don't actually have Jonathan's phone number and I can totally understand not picking up strange numbers. I get enough spam on my own phone that I rarely answer. I can only imagine how much worse it would be for someone with actual money to spend.

"Okay."

Christopher reaches into his pocket and pulls out his phone. He unlocks it, scrolls through his contacts, and hands it to me. I quickly memorize the number, just in case.

I hit dial and wait for the ringing.

"There's no change," Jonathan announces on the fourth ring. "Mom is still freaking out. You're going to have to switch with me soon, Christopher."

"It's not Christopher, it's me."

"Oh. Nora." The tone of his voice shifts from annoyed to friendly. "How are you? Are you okay? I'm sorry about yesterday and my brother."

He says something else, but the phone line crackles. I know that the reception at the hospital is spotty. Christopher is politely standing on my porch pretending to inspect some flowers in a pot. I don't believe he's interested in my pansies in the slightest though.

"Me, too." I'm suddenly not sure what I wanted to say. I can't confess my undying love over the phone with Christopher standing right there.

There's a loud screeching on the other side of the phone. I hear yelling and beeping.

"Can I call you back? My mother needs me," he announces, having to yell a little bit.

"Sure," I yell back. "We'll talk soon." The line goes dead.

"You good?" Christopher asks as I hand him back the phone.

I feel like I'm being set up. I feel like Mrs. Lewis is in on Christopher's plan to keep me away from Jonathan. I don't know how having a friend in the hospital plays into that, but I can't shake the feeling. It wouldn't really surprise me if it was a set up, but I don't like the feeling.

"Yeah. I just need to grab a few things. I'll be right back," I tell him, leaving him on the porch. I run inside and grab my swim things and a change of clothes. I'm already dressed in a cute pair of Capri pants and a flirty top that makes my cleavage look good. I was planning on visiting Jonathan and I wanted to look nice. Now, I guess it just makes traveling with Christopher that much easier. I send my dad a quick text that I'll be out late and not to worry about me.

I grab a light sweater from the back of a chair, shrugging into it as I open the front door. It takes me a minute to manage my bag and the door, but soon I'm standing on the landing to our apartment with Christopher.

"Are you cold?" Christopher asks, looking at my sweater.

"I'm used to being in the Caribbean," I explain as we

make our way down the stairs and cross the gardens to the main house. "It's warm here, but it's not tropical warm."

"I just need to grab some paperwork," Christopher says as he holds open the front door to the main house for me.

The house has always been grand. Everything is meant to impress guests with the wealth of the Lewis family. There's plenty of comfort, but the main goal of the house isn't for living in. It's for showing off the Lewis fortune. There are gilded picture frames, expensive vases, and all sorts of new technologies meant to make lives easier.

Given that it's just Deborah that lives here now, she has more than enough staff to not need the gadgets. Both Christopher and Jonathan have luxury apartments in the city and various beach houses throughout the world. The Lewis house is still the center of their orbit, but I can't see them staying here once Deborah passes away. This house is a relic of the boys' childhood.

Still, it smells like home to me. The scent the housekeepers use hasn't changed since I was a child. The air is cool with only the hum of the air conditioner and a vacuum running in a faraway room. Every once in a while a crystal chandelier tinkles when the air hits it just right.

Christopher leads the way to the main staircase. I know where Jonathan's room is. I've known for a long time. It's up the stairs and two doors to the right. Jonathan's room is three doors down from that.

I pause in front of the open door to Jonathan's room as Christopher keeps walking. I haven't been inside Jonathan's room since we were children. It's a place that holds mystery and promise. A place that I have to be invited.

I peek into the empty room, stealing a glimpse of the

forbidden. Inside the room is dark. The heavy curtains are pulled against the morning sunshine. The walls are clear of the posters Christopher used to have. Now, it looks like a guest bedroom. A large flat-screen TV hangs on the far side of the room.

Christopher emerges from his room with just a computer bag over his shoulder. "Ready?"

I know I should go, but something keeps me planted by the bedroom door. I have a connection to Jonathan here. I have a feeling that if I leave this room, Jonathan will forget all about me. The hope that he might finally see me, chose me, that I'd find love from the man I'd always wanted will disappear.

However, there's no reason for me to stay and every reason to go. There's a hotel management team with my name on it just waiting for me. There's just an empty room here.

"Nora? The plane's waiting." Christopher is standing by the stairs, checking his watch. He's ready to leave.

I look one last time at the room, wishing that Jonathan really was there. I want to talk to him. I think of our conversation in the restaurant and I ache for more of that. But there's nothing here for me. Not really.

I turn and walk away.

CHAPTER 7

The helicopter is waiting on the pad for us. The blades already whirl and spin as we approach, ready for us to take off.

"We're taking the helicopter?" I ask, sure Christopher had said something about a plane. I realize that I have no idea where we are going.

Christopher looks at the helicopter and then at me. "Saves time," he explains as if it should be obvious. "The plane's waiting for us at the tarmac."

I frown, wondering what a helicopter like this must cost and what the hell I have gotten myself into.

"What, you'd rather sit in traffic?" Christopher asks me.

With that he walks out to the helicopter, right under the blades, and steps inside. He doesn't duck as he walks. He doesn't look afraid. He walks into the helicopter the way I walk into a subway car. Like it's something I've done all my life.

I swallow hard and follow him. I duck low under the

swirling blades. They're noisy and I can feel the wind they make. I pull myself up the stairs and into the cabin of the helicopter.

It's small, but comfortable. The seats are leather and the windows are big. I sit down, unsure of what to do next.

Christopher yells something at me, but I can't hear him over the beating blades outside. I knew they were loud, but I didn't expect them to be this loud inside the helicopter. If fancy cars have noise canceling capabilities, why wouldn't fancy helicopters?

"What?" I shout back. Christopher points to the headset he's wearing and then to one resting a hook next to my seat. I grab it and put it on backwards the first time. It takes me a minute to get it right. I settle it on my head, glad for the quiet.

Next comes the seat-belt. Apparently, helicopters don't use regular seat-belts. They use fancy five-point harnesses that I have no idea how to use. They remind me of the straps on a baby's car seat.

Christopher leans over and helps me fasten the clips after watching me struggle for a few seconds.

"Haven't you ridden in a helicopter before?" he asks through the headset.

I shake my head. "Nope. First time."

"You have to push the button," he tells me, pointing to the headset. "Otherwise it doesn't transmit and I can't hear you."

I push the button this time. "Nope. First time."

Christopher wears surprise like it doesn't fit him. I suppose that being the CEO of a billion dollar company means that you always have to be prepared for anything. Surprise isn't something a CEO should experience often.

"Butler's daughter," I remind him, pointing to myself. "Not the pilot's daughter."

He doesn't push the button, but I can clearly see him breath out a "huh." He looks at me like I just told him that I've never eaten white bread.

I shake my head and look out the window. The helicopter rises and soars into the sky. It's surprisingly smooth and graceful. I'm grinning from ear to ear as we fly over the green trees and cars I've only ever seen from the ground. I see the Lewis house and the neighbors' estates, the pools and the golf course, and all the way out to the small private airport. I love every minute of it.

Helicopters are now my favorite way to travel.

Christopher has to show me how to unbuckle the the harness. I hang the headset up as neatly as I can, but it's still very obvious I have never done this before. I follow him out of the helicopter, and once again, he barely ducks under the blades. He walks with confidence toward a small jet waiting just across the tarmac.

I try to mimic his easy movements and fail miserably. I stumble out of the helicopter and practically crawl on my belly across the tarmac because I don't want those blades anywhere near my head. That's one part of helicopter travel that will take some getting used to.

Christopher waits for me at the bottom of the stairs to the jet. He's got this small smile on his face that I've never seen before.

"What?" I ask him, crossing my arms as I come up.

"You really haven't been on a helicopter before." He grins at me. "Have you been on a plane before?"

"Just the big ones," I tell him. "Do I have to pay for my drinks on yours? I'll have to pay you back for my baggage fee. You know it's cheaper to pay at check-in than at the gate."

Christopher chuckles at my poor attempt at a joke and sweeps his arm to the side, motioning me to go up the stairs into the plane. I grin at him as I go up the short ramp of steps and into the Lewis' private jet.

I stand in the doorway of the airplane and gape like a fool. This isn't an airplane. This is someone's living room. Someone's really expensive living room.

There are white leather recliners and even a couch. Everything looks comfortable and beautiful, especially when compared to the usual anchovy-can flights I usually fly.

"What do you think?" Christopher asks, a smug grin on his face as he comes up behind me.

"I guess you paid the extra for extended leg room."

He laughs. I'm glad to know I can make him laugh.

I choose one of the recliner chairs near a window. Christopher takes the matching seat across from me. There is a small table between us that looks like it can fold up into the wall when not in use, but right now it looks like a very trendy piece of furniture.

I know how to use the seat-belt in this airplane at least, and I easily click it into place around my waist.

"Something to drink?" A lovely woman in a blue traditional 1950's style stewardess dress asks me. She even has the hair and hat like the old-time stewardesses. She sets a bottle of chilled Peligrino water and a tall glass of ice in front of Christopher. He nods a polite acknowledgment at her.

"Um, what do you have?" I ask. I don't see one of the

drink menus in the back pocket of the seat in front of me. In fact, there is no seat in front of me. Just Christopher.

The stewardess smiles. "Just about anything you can want. Mr. Lewis has us keep everything fully stocked."

I consider having something alcoholic, but this is supposed to be a work trip.

"Lemonade?" I ask.

"Fizzy or flat?"

"There's fizzy lemonade?" I didn't know such a thing existed, but it sounds wonderful. "I'll take that."

She smiles and looks to Christopher.

"I'm good," he tells her. She nods and hurries to the back to get me my drink.

"Carbonated lemonade is common in Europe and Australia," Christopher informs me. "I keep it on board for my international clients."

"Oh. Well, then I feel very European and fancy," I reply. It's barely thirty seconds before the stewardess is back with my drink.

I sip at it, smiling at the way the carbonation bubbles tickle my nose. I like it. It's different than I expected, yet familiar at the same time. Somehow it's a combination of something comforting and exciting at the same time.

The plane begins to move. I hold onto my armrest during takeoff, but the flight up is surprisingly smooth. I'm far less nervous than I am on my regular flights. I suppose it's easier to feel comfortable when you don't have two babies crying, a couple fighting two rows over, and the man sitting next to you trying to tell you the benefits of his new rash cream.

"Here are the specs for the resort," Christopher says,

handing me a stack of paperwork. "It's small and very exclusive."

I flip through the file and try to ignore the numbers written on them. They are all very large with way too many zeros. However, the amenities and property look good.

"It looks promising," I say, turning a page. "How did you find it?"

"Jonathan was there not too long ago." Christopher watches me as I look up at him. He's sitting comfortably in his chair, one leg resting at the ankle on his knee. He looks comfortable and in control. I suppose he should since this is technically a business meeting and that's his life.

"He was?" I try not to put any emotion into my voice. I know Jonathan takes girls to exotic locations. It's part of his routine. I just never expected to go to one, and I certainly never even dreamed of going to one with Christopher instead.

"The bill caught my attention."

Must have been some bill to catch a billionaire's attention, I think to myself. Especially given the way Jonathan likes to spend money.

"So do you plan on buying it to save yourself some cash?" I ask. "I thought Jonathan was supposed to be getting married."

"Since Jonathan doesn't seem to care about the business or have a concept of money, yes." Christopher smiles at me. "It'll be a cheaper honeymoon, if nothing else."

We both look at each other, knowing that we're trying to push buttons and make the other flustered. For me, it's mentioning Jonathan actually getting married. For Christopher, it's that the wedding isn't happening.

Christopher's phone starts to ring. It's a traditional, old-school-phone sound that makes me smile. Of course Christopher would have something practical for his ringtone.

"Aren't you supposed to turn those off during a flight?" I ask, crossing my arms.

"Not if you're me. Excuse me." He answers his phone and goes straight into business.

It sounds important, but not terribly urgent. If nothing else, it assures me that this trip is a distraction, not an actual business transaction. If it were, Christopher would be telling me a lot more about the file I have in front of me.

"Yes, of course I'm managing things," Christopher says into the phone. He drops his voice and looks away from me. I pretend not to notice as I look out the window. "I'm doing everything I have to do. Nothing is more important. This is getting taken care of one way or another."

I pretend not to hear his words. I pretend not to know that he's talking about me and my relationship with his brother. The relationship I have wanted for so long. I pretend it doesn't sting that Jonathan's family doesn't think I'm not good enough.

I turn my attention back to the file in front of me. I don't need to listen to Christopher. I already know the reason I'm here and it's only partially to look at a resort. I flip through the file, pausing at the various images and descriptions of the rooms and services.

The resort is definitely extravagant. It's something that I would dream about running someday. It's small, yet has the capability to do big things. I'm used to being around people with money, so a resort like this feels comfortable to me. I know what to expect and how my guests expect to be treated.

I'm glad my name will be tied to this resort. If I had a couple million sitting in the bank, I might even ask Christopher if I could become a partial partner. However, I don't have a couple million. I barely have a couple hundred.

I wonder if Christopher is done with his phone conversation. I glance up and see that the phone is still at his ear.

"Damn, it's not in my pocket. Hold on." Christopher frowns as he pats around his pockets looking for something. He frowns as he find a pen in his back pocket. I raise my eyebrows at him. "I usually have a suit," he explains.

I smile and shake my head, going back to my file. When he's immersed in his conversation again, I sneak a glance at him. I still can't believe he's wearing slacks and a polo. I can't remember the last time I saw him in something so informal and comfortable. I didn't even know he owned clothes that weren't part of a suit.

It looks good on him. He looks less stern and imposing. If he could wear an actual t-shirt rather than a polo, he might even look relaxed. He might even look human.

Christopher frowns as he says something into his phone, but then he looks up and sees me watching him. He smiles at me. A real, actual smile.

It's short, but warm. It feels like sunshine. I like his smile.

I flush a little, and go back to looking at my papers. He has a great smile.

In fact, his smile might actually be better than Jonathan's.

CHAPTER 8

I finish my lemonade, but before I can even set the glass down, I have a fresh one.

When you are the only customer, the service is pretty amazing. It probably helps when the boss is flying with you, too.

Christopher finally finishes his business call. He looks to put the phone in a suit coat pocket, but since he's dressed casually, he has to adjust and put the phone in his pants. He looks awkward and annoyed.

"Sorry about that," he says as if we didn't just have a forty-five minute interruption. "Business."

"It's always business with you," I reply.

"That's my lot in life." He shrugs, but doesn't deny it. He motions to the file in my hands. "So, what do you think?"

"It looks like a great resort and hotel," I tell him. "I'm not sure if it's a great price, though. I'm afraid I don't know what private islands are going for these days."

"It's a seller's market," he says with a shrug.

"If the amenities are what they claim to be, it could be a good investment. The nearby ecology sanctuary is great. You'll need to look into the weather patterns. And getting staff there may be an issue." I flip through the file, looking at the specs of the island. It's small, but has a private airport. There is a small town nearby, but nothing major.

"So staffing would be your big concern?" he asks me.

I nod. "We always had problems recruiting staff due to the size of the island. Increasing pay tends to help, but it's more about the work environment being a good one." I look him in the eye. "Loyalty is everything in this business."

He slowly nods, his eyes coming to meet mine. They are a beautiful blue that reminds me of the Caribbean waters we're about to go visit.

"Thank you," he tells me.

I chuckle. "I haven't done anything yet."

"You're giving me an honest opinion. I appreciate that. You aren't selling me," he explains. "It's nice to know someone isn't trying to get something out of me. Instead, you're telling me what to expect."

"And you think I wouldn't?" I counter, crossing my arms. "Even though the reason you are whisking me away to a tropical island is to keep me away from your brother, I'm still going to tell you the truth. Even though this is obviously a set up, I'm going to pretend it's a job."

Christopher doesn't say anything. He just sips on his bubbly water, watching me. Anger flares hot in my stomach. I don't like that I'm being manipulated, even though I agreed to this.

"Does you have Adeline flying in to see him and

remind him of how much he loves her while I'm otherwise occupied?" I ask, venom in my voice.

Christopher just raises his eyebrows and takes another sip of water.

"What? Am I wrong?" There's annoyance in my voice now.

He carefully sets his glass down on a small square napkin. "I'm actually not calling Adeline to see him just yet. I don't want him to say something he can't take back."

I have to admit that makes sense. The last thing Christopher would want is for Adeline to come home and have Jonathan to tell her that they're through. Especially while Christopher's busy with me and unable to do damage control.

"You knew what this was?" Christopher asks. His posture is relaxed, but his attention is focused solely on me. It's a little intimidating to be the sole person in the gaze of Christopher Lewis.

"You randomly happened to have something that you knew I couldn't resist show up the very day you needed it to?" I shake my head. "The universe doesn't make coincidences like that."

Christopher gives a slow nod. "No. It usually hides them in plain sight." When I look at him to explain, he just waves his hand. "Tell me about the Caribbean. It's where you got the experience I need. Did you like living there?"

"I loved it."

"Did you miss anything from home?"

I think of Jonathan, but I don't say anything.

"Other than Jonathan, I mean," Christopher says, reading my mind.

"I missed the seasons. It's actually hard living in

paradise without anything to break up the days. I found I missed it getting cooler and the leaves changing color. I even missed snow, but not that much." I chuckle. "I haven't really missed snow. Just at Christmas."

Christopher smiles. "What else?"

"I love the beaches and the palm trees. I loved that I could go snorkeling every day if I wanted to. I actually learned how to scuba dive just so I could stay in that underwater world for a little bit longer."

"You're a mermaid. Like Ariel." He smiles at me and I'm reminded of Julie telling me that I'm Ariel as well.

"Except Ariel wanted to go to the human world, and I'd trade my voice to go to the mermaid world in a heartbeat," I reply. "It's a good deal for me because you don't really need a voice underwater."

"I've never been scuba diving," Christopher tells me.

"It's so much fun." I grin, remembering my time with the fish. "The world down there is so different and beautiful. It's everything I liked about snorkeling, but longer and and better."

Christopher shrugs. "I'm afraid I've never been snorkeling, either."

Now it's my turn to look surprised. How did Christopher never go snorkeling? I know his mother has a beach house in Hawaii and he's been to Australia enough times to practically be a citizen. "What? Seriously?"

He smiles at me and shakes his head. "We've been on trips to places I could go, but I was always busy with other things. It never seemed important."

My plan for the day starts to change. Since we're not really here on a business mission, we can have some fun.

If I'm going to be stuck with Christopher, we might as well enjoy ourselves.

"I guess this will be a day of firsts," I inform him. "I got to fly in a helicopter, you will go under the ocean."

"What do you mean?" I obviously caught him by surprise and it makes me smile.

"Since this trip is a tactic to keep me away from Jonathan, you get to take me snorkeling."

He points to the file of information on the resort. "No, you're here for the resort..."

"And we need to test the amenities and activities for ourselves. How else will you know what your guests will experience unless you try it for yourself?"

He has no counter argument. He opens his mouth and then closes it. He knows I have him unless he wants to admit to this being a complete sham. He's not willing to do that.

"I still have to get work done," he tells me.

"And if I sneak home and seduce your brother?" I ask. "It'll be easy. You just told me Adeline isn't home right now."

Christopher narrows his eyes at me. "You wouldn't."

I shrug, pretending like I might. I know that I would never do such a thing, but I can play the part. I can't believe I'm having to blackmail Christopher into having fun.

Christopher believes my bluff. His jaw clenches and then he sighs. "Fine."

"Be careful, Christopher," I warn with a grin. "You might actually have fun today. I'd hate for that to happen."

He shakes his head, annoyed, but there's a hint of a

smile near his mouth. I hope I can coax a real one out again. I want to see him smile for real.

Christopher's phone rings and he answers it instantly. More business. It's always business with Christopher. Our fun, playful banter is over while he debates deals over the phone. I sigh and look out the window at the swirls of clouds and sky. I am excited to introduce someone to the joys of snorkeling.

Hopefully, his phone doesn't work underwater.

CHAPTER 9

Blue skies and leafy green palm trees greet us.

I step off the plane and take a deep breath in. If I ignore the scent of jet fuel, I can almost smell the ocean. It's different here than in New York. The ocean here is lighter and more tropical. The sun is different here, too. There's more yellow and colors seem brighter.

A man in a dark blue suit is waiting for us at the base of the stairs. He's smiling as we carefully navigate the steps from the plane. Christopher leads. The wind whips at his brown hair and he squints in the sun.

"Mr. Lewis, your suite is prepared and ready for you. As requested, there is a fax machine and video conferencing equipment available in your room," the man says.

Christopher glances in my direction. I cross my arms. He's not getting out of this. He doesn't get to fly me out here and leave me on my own.

"Actually, that won't be necessary," Christopher tells the man. "I'll be accompanying Nora."

"Of course, sir." The man smiles and nods. "If you'll

come with me, we have fresh drinks for you in the limo. The resort is just a short drive. We hope you don't mind."

We follow the man across the hot tarmac and to the waiting limo. The cool leather seats stick slightly as I slide in. The humidity of the ocean is everywhere here. I shiver slightly at the air conditioned interior of the limo. There's a bucket of ice, heavy with condensation, chilling an open bottle of champagne. Two champagne flutes sit ready by its side.

"So you were going to abandon me today?" I ask Christopher, crossing my arms.

I hear the limo's engine rev and the car glides forward as the driver takes us to the resort.

"No." He manages to look innocent. Mostly.

I raise a skeptical eyebrow.

"Only for a little bit," he concedes. "There's just so much to do with the merger."

"You were going to ditch me." I shake my head and make a disappointed sound as I reach for the champagne. I look over at him and smirk. "No wonder you can't get a date."

"I get dates," he replies indignantly. "I don't know what my brother's been telling you."

"Business meetings don't count as dates," I tease him, pouring us both a glass of champagne.

"Ouch." He smiles at me though, taking the glass of champagne I offer him. "I do have dates. Plenty of them."

"Sure." I shrug, and sip at my champagne. It's fun to tease Christopher. I like that he smiles at me when I do it. I'm not sure many people tease the billionaire. In fact, I'm sure no one does. It's a shame, because Christopher actually does have a fun sense of humor.

"I go on dates," he assures me. "You ever hear of Meghan Markle? We dated. Recently."

"Oh? And how'd her husband like that?" I ask, managing to almost keep a straight face.

Christopher frowns. "What do you mean?"

"She married Prince Harry last year, and just had a baby," I inform him. "You must not have heard."

"Really?" He looks perplexed, and I can see him going over the timeline of the past year in his head. "You're sure?"

"Unless there's another Prince Harry of England, yeah. I'm pretty sure."

"Well, damn."

I shake my head at him. "When's the last time you relaxed and had fun'?"

"Work is fun." He shrugs like that should be obvious.

"Oh, Christopher." I roll my eyes a little. I should have remembered that business is all Christopher is.

Christopher frowns, his dark brows coming together softly. He looks contemplative, like he's figuring out a business opportunity. I can practically see the wheels spinning behind his blue eyes.

"What are you thinking?" I ask him. I'm suddenly a little nervous.

He reaches into his pocket and pulls out his phone. I try not to take it personally that he is going to take a business call in the middle of our conversation. Maybe he's calling Meghan Markle.

"Lucy?" he says. I seem to remember that's the name of his secretary. "Yes. I'm going dark. Forward everything to Mom. I'll check in at..." Christopher checks his watch. "In five hours. Mom can handle anything until then."

He clicks off the phone and then hands it to me. I take the phone into my hands. It's warm and heavy.

"Don't let me have it," Christopher tells me. "You're in charge of making sure I have fun today."

I look down at the sleek phone in my hands. I'm holding Christopher's world in my fingers, and he's trusting me. He's willing to take the risk. Slowly, I start to smile.

"Seriously?" I ask him. "You'll do whatever I want today?"

"Within reason." He looks nervous as my grin spreads. He laughs uneasily. "And now I'm suddenly regretting this decision."

I tuck the phone carefully into my bag. "Christopher, we are going to have a good time today."

If he's going to keep me away from Jonathan, I'm at least going to enjoy myself here. I'll make sure that Christopher has a good time too.

CHAPTER 10

The limo stops and we get out at paradise.

I can hear the soft song of the ocean. Birds call overhead and the wind caresses the palm trees. The world is warm and made of liquid sunshine and green plants. I love the islands.

A woman in a suit with a name tag comes out to greet us. Behind her is a large open air lobby. The building is made out of local materials, giving it a very tropical tiki look. The decorations inside are a subdued tropical design that reminds me of a fancy spa I once went to.

"Welcome to the Ocean Retreat. My name is Anna and I'm here to help you with anything you need." Her bright smile is warm and welcoming. "If you'll follow me, I'll take you to your room."

I grin over at Christopher as she motions us to walk through the lobby and out onto a boardwalk. The lobby is cool with fans blowing softly. There's several comfortable chairs and a large check-in area. A man stands at the desk and smiles politely as we pass.

I gasp as we cross the boardwalk. It's an over-water resort. There are two boardwalk paths leading out into the ocean. Thatched roof bungalows are carefully interspersed along the boardwalk, but they are on stilts over the water. We will be staying in a room that is in the middle of a tropical lagoon.

We walk down to the far end of one of the paths. The smell of clean ocean air and tropical flowers is refreshing and wonderful. I take a deep breath in and feel my soul lighten. For the first time in days, I feel warm.

Anna leads us to the farthest bungalow. It's made of what looks like bamboo and thatch, but it looks sturdier than that. I expect that it's made of more modern materials, but designed to look natural and tropical.

Inside the bungalow is beautiful. A huge, bigger-than-king-size bed with white linen dominates the room. Massive windows dominate the right hand wall, opening up to show the entire expanse of the lagoon. To the left is a comfortable looking white linen couch, a chair, and two doors.

The first door leads to a small sitting room with huge windows looking at the lagoon and toward the far beach. Palm trees dot the white sand beach and there are several lounge chairs with happy looking people sunning themselves in the distance. A fax machine and video conference equipment sits on a small desk near the window. It looks out of place against the the blue Caribbean water, white billowy curtains, and spa-like furniture. Work doesn't belong in a place like this.

The other door leads to the bathroom. It's huge. Bigger than two of my father's bathrooms put together. There is a large claw-foot tub with a window overlooking the water outside. The shower starts out inside, but there is a removable panel that leads outside as well, making it an indoor/outdoor shower. I count at least five shower heads.

It's basically bathroom heaven.

I go back to the main room where Anna is standing by the door out to the deck. She stands with her hands politely clasped in front of her, waiting for us to be ready.

I step past her and out onto the deck. It's made with the plastic wood that looks like real wood. I like this because it means there won't be splinters. There is a shaded thatch roof over the first part of the deck. Two wicker chairs with linen cushions rest in the shade with a large table for eating. A tiki bar is to the side, and I can see it's fully stocked. Outside the shaded area is a small infinity pool that butts up to the ocean. To the side of that, there's a sitting space with a metal ladder leading from the edge of the deck into the ocean. I could jump off the edge of the deck, swim with the fish, and come back up to the porch for dinner.

Anna and Christopher join me on the deck.

"For all meals, we have a gourmet chef available. There is someone in the kitchen at all hours," Anna explains. She motions to the side of the bungalow where I see a white telephone and a menu tucked cleverly into a discrete space. "We are happy to have meals prepared ahead of time or as requested. There is a menu of the chef's specialties, but please feel free to make requests. Our kitchen is fully stocked."

I go over and peek at the menu. Everything looks amazing. My mouth starts to water at the descriptions and I realize I'm starting to get hungry.

"Along with the menu, there are also a list of amenities

and activities available. If you would like, I can arrange for various activities for you," Anna offers.

"Is the snorkeling good around here?" I ask.

Anna nods. "There is wonderful snorkeling just off your deck here. The fish like to hide in the shade of the bungalows, but if you want the best snorkeling, I recommend the local coral reef. It's on the far side of the lagoon."

"That sounds amazing. How do we get there?"

"We have a glass bottom boat that goes there. It's very close. The reef has some of the best snorkeling in the world. We just had a National Geographic film-crew there a few weeks ago." Anna smiles at me. "Would you like me to arrange it?

Anna reminds me of my father. The woman knows how to present herself like a true butler. She is making sure that her clients are completely cared for without being pushy or too forward. It's a difficult skill to perfect.

"Thank you," I tell her. "I'd like to look at all the options first."

"Of course, ma'am." Anna bobs her head in deference. She looks between Christopher and me. "If you need anything, please don't hesitate to call. There are telephones in every room with my direct line. We'd like to make your stay perfect."

"Thank you," I say, tucking the food menu back into its place. "This looks wonderful."

Anna nods and excuses herself, leaving me and Christopher alone in paradise.

"So, what do you think?" Christopher looks around the back deck.

"I'm curious why there's only one bed," I tease him,

pointing to the room. "What kind of girl do you think I am?"

I know that this is meant to be a day trip and we were never planning on using the bed. Still, it is too good an opportunity to pass up to tease him.

Christopher looks at the room and shrugs. "It's a big bed. Besides, do you know how expensive this place is? I'm not getting you your own room. I have to save money somewhere."

I laugh, enjoying that he's teasing me back. I'm already enjoying this trip more than I thought I would. Christopher hasn't been nearly as bad as I was afraid he would be.

Christopher grins at me and I'm caught off guard. He's incredibly handsome when he smiles. It's like the world lights up. There's a sparkle in his eyes and the way his mouth curves is amazing. I feel my girl parts react as well since the gaze is directed at me.

And that's unexpected.

"This is beautiful," I say, turning away and facing the water so he can't see the effect he's having on me. "I didn't know there was an over-the-water bungalow place like this in the Caribbean. I've seen pictures of the ones in Bora Bora, but this is amazing."

"The over-the-water bungalows are a newer addition," he informs me. "There's a regular hotel and private bunga- lows on the shore as well."

I nod. "That makes sense."

I'm waiting for my heart to stop thudding in my chest. I didn't expect to ever think Christopher was attractive. I mean, I always thought he was handsome, but thinking it and experiencing attraction to him because of it, are two very separate things.

"What would you like to do first?" Christopher asks, looking around at the lagoon.

I can tell that laying poolside doing nothing would drive him crazy. Christopher is a doer. He doesn't know how to sit down and relax. Trying to get him to sit in the sun and enjoy doing nothing would have him hugging the fax machine for dear life in about twenty minutes. I need to ease him into this vacation thing.

"Let's see," I say, going back to the menu. I pick up the one with things to do and begin to leaf through it. There's a wonderful assortment that caters to just about every activity level a person could want. There's in-room spa options with everything from massages to facials to mud baths. There's the typical ocean activities of glass bottom boat, ski-dos, parasailing, scuba diving, and deep sea fishing. There's private tai chi lessons, yoga, SUP (stand up paddle board), yoga on SUP, cooking options, and more. There's even a list at the end of things at the onshore resort to do- a movie theater, a bowling alley, swimming pools with slides, and tennis courts.

However, I know what we're going to do.

I pick up the white phone. There's a soft beep on the other end and a voice instantly asking, "how may I help you?"

"Hi, I'd like to order the starfish package," I tell the voice.

"Of course. And the cuisine?'

"Caribbean. Anything that's local, please."

"When would you like it?"

"Now-ish?" I ask. "We need to change first, but as soon as possible."

"Of course, ma'am. I can have the boat arrive at your bungalow in ten minutes if that's acceptable?"

"Yes, thank you." I like this place. They're good. They're very good.

The voice verifies with me that the starfish package will be there in approximately ten minutes and then politely hangs up. I'm very impressed with the service here so far.

"Alright. Get changed into your swim trunks," I tell Christopher. "We're going on an adventure."

He nods and walks into the bedroom. He stops at the bed and turns around.

"I didn't bring swim trunks," he informs me. "I planned on working."

"Then I guess you go naked, because you aren't getting out of this," I tease. I make a show of looking him up and down, like I'm imagining him naked. I like the way his cheeks pink just a little.

I go to the white phone in the bedroom this time and pick it up. Once again, the voice on the other end is nearly instant.

"Hi, do you have swim trunks we can use?" I ask.

"Of course, ma'am," the voice tells me. "What size would you like?"

I look over at Christopher. He's tall and lean. While I can imagine him naked, I'm having a hard time figuring out a size. Probably because I'm too busy imagining him naked.

"Whatever size Jonathan usually wears when he's here is fine," I tell the voice.

"Of course, ma'am. I'll walk them over myself." The phone clicks off and I hang up.

Christopher looks over at me. "How did you know Jonathan would have swim trunks here? I know I mentioned he'd come here once, but that seems like a jump."

"This is something Jonathan would set up," I tell him. "He wouldn't come here just once. This place is perfect for seducing a woman, especially on short notice. I'm guessing you called his secretary and just had her set up whatever he normally gets. The one bed is kind of the giveaway."

"It's all she ever does," Christopher says with a chuckle. "She did give me options, though. I thought you would like this better than Martha's Vineyard."

I cock my head to the side. "Why wouldn't I like Martha's Vineyard?"

"You said you were cold since coming home," Christopher explains. "It was supposed to rain there today."

I'm surprised he was paying attention. I smile at him, feeling a grateful warmth at the fact that he remembered something about our conversation. "Yes, this is better. Thank you."

Christopher shrugs. One side of his mouth curves up in a smile as he looks around. "I have to admit, Jonathan does have good taste."

I nod, looking around the room. The sky and ocean look almost fake they're so perfect and blue out the windows. I can hardly believe a place this beautiful exists, let alone that I'm staying here as a guest.

"Are you really thinking of buying this place?" I ask. "Or was that a lie to get me here?"

"It really is for sale," he tells me. "Jonathan wants Paris for a honeymoon, but this would save on his weekend getaways."

The fact that Jonathan is getting married should hurt more, but right now, it doesn't bother me. I'm surprised that I'm not upset at Christopher mentioning it.

Before I can think on that further, there's a soft knock at the front door. I hurry over and find Anna with three different swim trunks in her arms. They all still have their tags and they all have designer labels.

"Mr. Lewis keeps these on hand. I also brought a size up and down, just in case," she explains.

"Thank you." She nods politely and disappears back down the boardwalk.

I close the door and turn to Christopher. "Do you want the bathroom or the bedroom?"

"For what?" He raises his eyebrows, confused.

"To change," I explain. "I know we grew up together and everything, but I'm not ready to get naked with you. Even if there is only one bed."

"Right. Right." His cheeks pink ever so slightly again as he grabs the trunks from my hand and ducks into the bathroom.

I shake my head and chuckle as I go to my bag and pull out my swim suit. It's a tasteful bikini that I picked up in the islands. It's actually a racing suit, so it stays in one place even in the ocean, but still looks like a bikini. It's cute, sporty, and fun. Perfect for today.

"You can come out whenever," I tell the bathroom door. "I'm all changed."

Christopher comes out a second later wearing one of the swim trunks. I try not to stare, but I find myself enjoying the sight of him. He's surprisingly fit for working in an office all day. Lean muscles, strong arms, and a defined chest are easy to see now that he's wearing nothing but a swimming suit.

He is super pale though. That part of being in an office all day is easy to see.

"You're going to want sunscreen," I tell him, forcing myself to look away from his body.

"There's some in the bathroom," he replies. He turns around and then comes back with a large bottle of coral reef safe sunscreen.

"I'll get your back if you get mine," I offer. I don't really have another way to keep my back from burning. I could call Anna, but I find myself thinking that Christopher will do a fine job. I try to ignore the thrum of excitement the idea of him touching me brings.

He hands me the sunscreen and we both go out to the back porch. He sits on a bench near the bar, his back to me. I pour the lotion in my hands and carefully rub it together to warm it.

His back is firm and strong as I rub the lotion into his skin. I can't help the little tingle of desire that flutters through me at touching him. He's an attractive man, even if he is Christopher.

"All done," I tell him, my voice cracking slightly. I quickly turn around so that he won't see my blush. I don't want Christopher to think that I'm hitting on him or that I'm trying to seduce him.

His hands are gentle as he works the lotion onto my back. I find myself relaxing into his touch and my shoulders loosening as his fingers massage the lotion into my skin. I close my eyes, enjoying the sensation. I don't want him to stop touching me. I don't want his hands to leave my skin.

My eyes open and I pull away when I realize that. "Thanks," I tell him. "That's good."

I step to the side and finish applying the sunscreen to the rest of my body. My thoughts are racing. Why is my heart pounding? Why am I hot and bothered? Why do I want him to keep touching me?

It's his brother I want. Right?

CHAPTER 11

"The boat's here," Christopher says, clearing his throat and pointing.

I look up in surprise. I thought we still had a few more minutes alone. Time went faster than I expected. Especially since I was contemplating telling Christopher I needed more sunscreen on my back.

I greet the boat driver and he helps me climb aboard. Christopher is right behind me. The boat is small with a seat in the back and on the sides. Right now, the two side benches have snorkeling gear and a cooler on them, taking up most of the sitting space. The bottom center of the boat is made of glass and we can see all the way down to the bottom of the ocean. Fish dart beneath my feet. I point them out to Christopher and he grins.

We sit next to one another on the small bench at the back. There isn't a lot of room in this small boat. Our legs are touching and once again, I can't stop thinking about his touch. I try to look around at the beautiful lagoon and not concentrate on his half naked body next to me.

The driver takes his seat at the front of the boat and slowly motors us away from the bungalow. The breeze is cool off the lagoon and my hair streams out behind me. I grin, loving being out on the clear blue water.

The boat hits a small bump and I reach out to steady myself. My hand comes down on Christopher's upper thigh. Heat sears through me. He has strong legs and my hand is closer to his groin than it should be.

"Sorry," I say, pulling my hand back and flushing red. I can still feel the searing heat from his leg pulsing through my hand and coursing into my body, particularly my girl parts.

"You're fine," he assures me with a chuckle. His blue eyes sparkle as he grins at me. "Grab me all you want. I'm here for you to experience the Lewis wooing. It's what my brother would be doing if he were here. It seems only fair."

The blush burns hot across my face and I'm glad there's a breeze or I'm afraid my cheeks might burst into flame. I don't want to think about Jonathan right now. It doesn't feel right to think about the other brother now. Not with Christopher smiling at me like that.

"So, what exactly is the starfish package?" Christopher asks, shifting the conversation away from his brother. He leans back and stretches his arm out to steady himself on the boat. His arm is behind me, but not holding me. He's not even touching me, but I find myself wishing that he was. I suddenly hope the boat hits another bump so that he'll have to wrap his arm over my shoulder.

"It's a glass bottom boat ride to the reef, snorkeling, and lunch," I reply, forcing my brain to stop concentrating on his well muscled arm behind me.

"Sounds good," he says with a smile. He looks out at the ocean and I can see his shoulders relax. The wind ruffles his hair and he closes his eyes, enjoying the sun like a cat. It's hard to have a conversation while the boat is in motion, so I just watch the water fly under our feet. Slowly the bare sand starts gathering rocks and fish until we're at the reef.

The boat driver kills the engine at the edge of the reef. I can already see hundreds of fish in the brightly colored world below.

"The snorkel goes on like this, and you breathe through it. If you get water in it, just blow out hard," I explain. "If you want to dive down deeper, you can pressurize your ears by holding your nose and blowing out. Do you need a life vest?"

Christopher adjusts the snorkeling mask over his eyes and grins. He looks so goofy and un-businesslike that I can hardly believe it's Christopher under the mask. Despite the fact that he looks like a deep-sea creature, he's never looked more human.

"I'm actually a pretty decent swimmer," he tells me. And with a grin, he jumps into the crystal blue water.

I'm only a couple of seconds behind him. The water is warm, like a tepid bath. Fish of blues and grays swirl around us, investigating and curious. They flash silver and bright as they swim past, unconcerned with their human guests.

Christopher is a natural and figures out the snorkel mask in no time. He floats calmly on the gentle waves, watching the world below with wonder. It's magic watching him discover this world for the first time and I'm so glad I convinced him to come along with me.

We swim side by side. I point out the various fish and corals. I even find an eel and we dive down a few feet for a closer look. The fish swirl around us like we belong there. This is where I feel most like I could be a mermaid.

Christopher grabs my hand and my heart speeds up. It's not because I think he sees a shark or something dangerous, my heart is pounding because he's touching me. A shark is less frightening than the way my body is reacting to his touch. I like being touched by him, and that, in some ways, is more dangerous than any ocean animal.

Christopher points out into the water and I see why he grabbed my hand. It's not a shark, but a sea turtle heading our way. I know the turtles in the Caribbean are gentle giants, so I grin at him around my snorkel and pull his hand to follow me.

We dive deeper into the water, holding our breath and filling our snorkels to say hello to the green turtle. The turtle watches us with ancient, calm eyes. They are deep and dark like the ocean, but gentle. It munches on some sea kelp, unconcerned with the silly humans.

We go back up for air and dive down again. Christopher is entranced by the turtle. We watch it gracefully meander along a patch of sand, searching for tasty green morsels of kelp or seaweed. A stingray glides by, and I can see Christopher's amazed face. His eyes go wide as the stingray leaves us and the turtle for deeper water.

He's still holding my hand. I don't want to let go, and not because I'm afraid we'll be separated by the current. I like holding onto him, even though it's doing strange things to my heart. I like him here with me under the water. Without the business suit and phone, I'm actually enjoying his humor and wit. He's funny and inquisitive.

His enthusiasm about exploring the reef is genuine and sweet.

I've never thought of Christopher like this before, but the more we're together, the more human and real he becomes.

It's in stark contrast to Jonathan. Jonathan is still perfect, almost too perfect to be real. I can't see Jonathan's flaws because I don't want to see them. I already know Christopher's flaws and I'm seeing past them.

We swim back to the boat after a while. It's more because we're both hungry than because there's nothing left to see. We could stay all day at the reef and never grow tired of it. However, my stomach is growling and so is Christopher's.

"That was amazing," Christopher says, flopping into the boat. He takes off his mask, leaving a big red mark where it pressed into his skin. He's grinning from ear to ear. "Did you see that stingray? And those little blue and purple fish?"

I laugh, enjoying his delight. "I'm glad you liked it," I tell him. I stand in the middle of the boat, wrapping a towel around my torso. I hand him a towel from the stack near the unused snorkel masks.

He drops onto the bench, wiping his face with the towel. "Liked it? I loved it."

He sighs with pleasure, leaning back against the back of the boat, his eyes closed and grinning. He squints one eye open against the bright sun, the grin still plastered on his face. The red goggle marks change his serious face into something much more friendly as he smiles at me. "Thanks for this."

"My pleasure," I tell him, matching his grin.

He scoots to the side of the bench, giving me room to sit. We wrap ourselves in towels, and the wind dries our hair as we coast back to our bungalow. We watch the fish dart beneath our boat as we leave the reef and then the desert stretch of sandy bottom until we're back to our place. There, fish are once again hiding in the shadows and venture under the boat.

Lunch is waiting for us at the outdoor table. There's more food than two people could ever or should ever hope to eat. Fresh local fruits, shrimp ceviche, fried plantains, fish tacos, jerk chicken skewers, rice, conch fritters, as well as bags of chips just in case that isn't enough food. And that isn't including the desserts. There are cookies and at least two kinds of cake.

"How many people are they thinking they need to feed?" I ask, walking across the deck and staring at awe at all the food. Sitting neatly on the two chairs are two fluffy robes with the resort's insignia on the breast pocket.

Christopher looks at the food and shrugs. "Looks normal to me."

I give him a surprised look. There is enough food here to easily feed six or more people. At my old job, I never handled the food, just the hotel side of things. I thought I was used to the way the rich and famous are treated, but this is more than I'm used to.

"You have a strange sense of normal," I tell him.

My skin is sticky with saltwater and I don't want to get salt all over the robe. I remember the outdoor shower and go around to the side of the deck. I turn on the shower, letting the freshwater wash over me. It feels good to get the skin-crackling salt off of me and out of my hair. I finish and turn the water off, looking for a fresh towel. I see one on the inside part of the bathroom, and go that way.

And I run into Christopher.

"Sorry," he says, taking a step back. "I was waiting for you to finish so I could shower."

"No, it's fine." I try and move to my left, and he goes to his right, effectively blocking me. We try again, and mirror one another once more. It's a silly dance of trying to pass one another and failing miserably.

Christopher laughs.

"Okay. You go that way, I'll go this way." Christopher has a playful smile that I've never seen before. If I didn't know better, I would think that Christopher is flirting with me.

I didn't know Christopher was capable of flirting.

I successfully navigate around a laughing Christopher and head back out to the deck. I hear the water turn on and I can hear it splash against Christopher's body. I try not to think about how good he looks wet, instead focusing on putting on my robe and figuring out what I want to eat.

Christopher joins me after a few minutes, his hair sticking up in odd angles from where he's dried it with his towel. He also puts on his fluffy robe, sighing with contentment as he takes a seat and starts putting food on his plate. He pops a piece of fruit in his mouth and sighs with contentment.

"Try the mango," he advises, wiping juice from his chin. "It's really good."

I point to my plate. "I'm already there." Most of my plate is already covered in fresh, juicy mango. I have other foods on there, but mango dominates my plate.

"I'm guessing you like mango," he says, putting another bite in his mouth.

I nod. "It's so good when it's fresh like this," I tell him. "There was this mango tree right outside of my apartment. We had so many mangoes, we couldn't possibly eat them all. I was eating them with a spoon like they were ice cream."

He takes another bite. "I have to admit, I usually don't like mango, but this is good."

"Fresh mango is so much better than what you can get in the store," I tell him. "I tried to get some for my dad, but it just wasn't the same. They don't travel well."

"You can have all the mango you want here," he tells me with a smile.

"Thank you." I set my fork down. "And I mean, thank you for more than just the mango. This has been a really nice day."

Christopher smiles at me, one of his rare, shining smiles that lights up the world. It's breathtaking and addicting. I wish he would smile like that all the time. I'd probably love him even more than Jonathan if he did.

"You're welcome." He looks around, appreciating the view and the comfortable bungalow. "This is pretty amazing."

"You should probably give Jonathan's secretary a raise for finding it," I tell him.

"Eh, it's all she has to do." His smile fades. "Maybe you can answer this. You seem to understand the inner workings of Jonathan's mind more than most. Why is he the way he is?"

"What do you mean?"

"I mean, he has a degree in business. He has an office in my building." Christopher frowns and pushes away his plate. "He has the experience, the pedigree, and the ability. I've seen some of his proposals and they're good. When he wants something, he gets it. He's more determined than I am sometimes."

I chuckle. "And you say I'm the Jonathan expert. Sounds like you know plenty about him."

He rolls his eyes just a little at me. "But why doesn't he use any of it?" Christopher shakes his head. "If you were in his shoes, would you do what he does? Always backing out of everything at the last minute? Why is it that all his secretary has to do is plan his dates? Why doesn't he use the talent that I know is in there?"

I finish a piece of mango, licking my fingers. I take my time, trying to figure out the best way to say this. Finally, I give up and just look at Christopher.

"It's because of you," I tell him.

Christopher frowns, pulling his head back. "What?"

"Look at you, Christopher." I motion to him sitting in front of me. "You're the perfect businessman."

"I'm wearing swim trunks," he reminds me. "And a fluffy robe."

"You know what I mean," I say with a chuckle. "You know exactly how to run the company. You've lined up this merger and all Jonathan had to do was date a girl for a little bit. What does Jonathan even have to do for the company? What can he do that you or your mother aren't already doing?"

Christopher doesn't say anything. I can see he's thinking it over, trying to understand what I'm saying.

"Do you remember his high school graduation party?"

I ask, trying to think of a way to demonstrate this idea to Christopher.

"He drank a whole bottle of wine and threw up in the pool," Christopher recalls. He doesn't look pleased at the memory.

"Yup, that's the party. But before he stole the wine, he was out greeting guests," I tell him. "One of the guests asked him what he was going to do next. He asked if Jonathan was going to take over the business."

"What did he say?" Christopher asks.

"Jonathan told him no. 'Why would I', he said. 'Christopher already has it taken care of. I'm the younger brother. It's my job to party.'"

Christopher scoffs. "Sounds just like something he'd say."

"He didn't say it flippantly," I explain. "He was sad. That's when he went and stole the wine. Don't you see? He has been living in your shadow his whole life."

"Could have fooled me." Christopher takes a long breath through his nose. His eyes cut back to me. "Did you go to that party?"

"No. I've never actually been a guest at one of your parties," I tell him.

"Then how do you know all this?" There's the hint of a skeptical businessman in his voice. I try not to take it personally.

"Because I was still there. I was helping park cars that day. I heard all of it. I may not be a part of your rich world but I have worked in it. I lived on those grounds the same as you. Just because I wasn't invited doesn't mean I wasn't there. I park cars, I trim grass, I serve drinks. I was always watching him. I wanted to be a part of your world so badly that I took every opportunity to be near it."

"A part of Jonathan's world," he corrects me, shaking his head.

I nod, my eyes going to my feet. Julie wasn't wrong when she called me Ariel. If I could have had a Jonathan statue, I would have hid it in a secret cave and talked to it just like she does in the movie.

"Did you ever watch me?" There's a tension in Christopher's voice that makes me look up at him. My chest tightens and I wish I had been watching him. Even just a little bit. It feels like I might have been missing out on something. Something wonderful.

Instead, I tell him a different truth.

"I would have, but I couldn't see you in your office."

CHAPTER 12

"What should we do now," Christopher asks. "Shopping? Isn't there a jewelry store on the property?"

We've finished lunch and are just sitting at the table, snacking on food we don't really need to eat but eating it because it's there.

The sun beats down on the thatched roof, but the breeze off the ocean lagoon keeps us comfortable in the shade. I don't really have a desire to move, besides, I'm not really into jewelry. I know I'm here to keep me away from Jonathan. I don't need to be bought off in addition to being distracted.

"I don't want your money, Christopher," I tell him. "You don't have to buy me things."

"You'd be the first," he replies.

"Then you need different dates."

Christopher looks thoughtful. I shake my head a little at him. I stand up and stretch my arms before going over to the menu of things to do. There's so many options.

Massages, bowling, fishing, jet skis, even something called water golf. They all sound too active or include other people. I'm comfortably full and very happy just sitting here in the bungalow.

I put the menu away and face Christopher.

"What if we just lay out here on the deck and enjoy the view?" I ask him.

"It's an excellent view," he tells me, but he looks at me when he says it, making me wonder if he's trying to flirt again. "But are you sure you want my company? I'm not very interesting. Jonathan's the interesting one."

"Are you trying to weasel your way into going back to work?" I ask him, crossing my arms. "Because I'm not giving you your phone back. You're stuck enjoying an afternoon relaxing with me."

"You sure you don't want to go shopping?" he offers. "Massage? Helicopter ride? I hear there's a shark sanctuary near here. I know the billionaire that supports it-"

"Christopher," I interrupt him. "If you don't want to spend time with me, just say so. You don't have to buy me off."

My heart catches at the thought that he might say he doesn't want to be here. I'm not sure why it bothers me. I've never had a thing for Christopher. I can't remember us actually spending time together in the past ten years, but I find myself enjoying our time here now. I'm *really* enjoying his company.

The breeze ruffles his dark hair. His shoulders are already turning pink from the sun, but they are more relaxed than I've seen in a long time.

"We'll need more sunscreen," he informs me with a

soft smile. I grin, glad that he's agreed to just relax here on the deck with the sound of the ocean all around us.

I walk over to the small tiki bar and start exploring our drink options.

"Daiquiri or margarita?" I ask him, looking through the various types of alcohol. Everything is in the little liquor bottles that the airlines give out.

"Neither?" he asks hopefully. "Can you make a martini?"

"Uh uh." I shake my head. "We're relaxing on the beach. We need beach drinks."

"We're not actually on the beach," he informs me with a smug smile. I stick my tongue out at him and he chuckles. "Whatever you're having."

"Well, there's no blender," I inform him. "So, margaritas on the rocks it is."

"No blender?" Christopher shakes his head. "Tsk, tsk. That's a point in the negative for this place."

"You should get a million dollars off the asking price," I reply, pouring out our drinks. "At least. Blenders are important things."

He laughs and my heart does the flippy-flop thing again. *How does he have such a good laugh?* I ask myself. *Probably from never using it. It's all stored up and powerful.*

I walk over to the table and hand him his drink. Then I motion him out onto the deck. Christopher finds a large beach umbrella that attaches to the dock so we have a little bit of shade. While he sets that up, I pile some food onto a plate and bring it over to us. I set it behind where we'll sit so we can snack at our leisure.

We sit at the edge of the deck, our feet in the ocean.

We're sitting close together, but not as close as we were sitting on the boat. Plus, there's no real chance of bumps, so I don't have a reason to touch him. That disappoints me for some strange reason.

The bright blue water is cool on our feet, the tropical sun hot everywhere else. I'm glad he found the umbrella to give us some shade. I close my eyes, tip my head back and smile at the sky. This is the good life.

"Look, dolphins," he cries, grabbing my shoulder.

I open my eyes and look out toward the water. Out where the water turns dark is a pod of three or four dolphins. They play in the waves, gliding and jumping over one another. It looks like so much fun, I can hardly look away. I glance over at Christopher to see him mesmerized.

"I haven't seen dolphins in years," he murmurs. "I never seem to have the time anymore."

We watch them until they disappear back into the deep blue water. It's like saying goodbye to an old friend. Still, I'm not sad. Not with Christopher there. He's an old friend too.

"Do you still have that red Corvette?" I ask after a while. The memory of him being an old friend brought it to me.

Christopher looks thoughtful. "I do, actually. That was my first car. I'm surprised you remember it."

"Do you remember that time you found me at the Robertson's party?" I ask him. "I was sixteen and drunk. You dragged me out of there and drove me home."

He chuckles and looks over at me. "You puked in my car."

"I did?" My mouth opens in embarrassment. "Oh god.

I don't remember that part. I don't remember a lot about that night to be honest."

"It wasn't much puke," he comforts me. "You managed to get it mostly out of the window. You were so apologetic. You tried to clean my car off with your sweater when we got home."

I grimace. I very vaguely remember that part. It wasn't my best night.

"I don't think I ever said thank you for that," I tell him. "And for not telling my dad."

He shrugs. "It was nothing."

"No, it wasn't." I reach over and touch his knee. It's not much, but he looks at me. "You didn't have to rescue me from that party."

"Yes, I did. Robertson's an ass. He liked to invite 'poor' girls to his house, get them drunk, take advantage of them, and then pay them off because they couldn't afford a lawyer. It was a sick game to him." There's a dark anger to his voice and his eyes flash. "I couldn't let him do that to you."

I look down at the water. I'd heard rumors of Robertson doing things to the not-rich girls. I always thought they were just rumors. I'd been so excited when he'd invited me to the party as his guest. I was finally going to be one of the cool kids. Even though I wasn't rich, I finally was going to be one of them.

It was stupid and I was lucky Christopher was there to rescue me. I shudder to think what might have happened to me if he hadn't dragged me out of the party.

I look down at my feet in the water. "So, is that why you punched him at the country club the next day?"

"He also made fun of my car," Christopher replies. I

look over at him. He's leaning back on his elbows, looking out at the water. The tips of his nose and ears are red and it's probably time to put on more sunscreen.

I suspect that the punch wasn't about the car. Christopher has a good heart. He used to care about people, but business got in the way. He let the cold businessman take control of his life. I wonder what happened to the sweet teenage boy I once knew. It's almost like he's here with me rather than the businessman Christopher's become.

"Thank you," I tell him, not pressing the issue. "It's a few years late, but thank you."

"You're welcome." He smiles at me. "It was a little weird explaining why my car was so clean to Jeff the next day."

"Jeff... the chauffeur before Craig?" I ask, trying to remember the names of people. "How was the car clean?

"After you went to bed, I cleaned it," Christopher explains. "I found the hose and soap and everything."

"Oh no!" I feel more guilty now than I did ten years ago. "You should have let me clean it off with my sweater."

Christopher laughs. "You were so drunk you weren't even cleaning the right spot. It was easier for me to do it."

"Now I really feel terrible," I say, shaking my head. "You drove me home, I puked in your car, and you cleaned it up?"

He laughs. "Don't worry. It wasn't my first time cleaning up that car."

"Oh. Well, then I feel far less special."

Christopher chuckles and the sound warms me better than the Caribbean sun. I never would have imagined sitting on a dock with Christopher would be so pleasant. I'm thoroughly enjoying myself.

"Do you remember when Mom had that summer party and the water fountain display went haywire?" Christopher asks. He smiles as he speaks, his eyes bright with memories.

I laugh remembering that summer. I ask if he remembers the dog that got loose on the property that one of the maids wanted to make the house pet.

We sit on the deck, our feet slowly kicking the water to nowhere. We reminisce about big events and house staff that have come and gone. It's like being with a long forgotten friend. We remember so many of the same people and things, just from different perspectives.

I can't believe that I'm sitting here with Christopher, talking like we're old friends. And that it feels so good and natural. There's no lag in conversation, no awkward pauses. It's just the two of us catching up and finding out that we actually have similar taste in books and movies.

It's quite possibly the strangest, and most wonderful, afternoon I have ever spent with a billionaire.

CHAPTER 13

Two margaritas later and we're still sitting on the dock laughing. The sun is starting to set, but we haven't run out of things to say or funny stories to tell. I feel like we never will.

I'm sure we're supposed to be heading back to the airplane soon, but I don't want to leave. I'm having such a good time with Christopher here on this dock. Every so often we see dolphins. Christopher loves them. They make him smile and laugh every time.

It's been the perfect day. One that I never expected, but enjoyed completely. If this is what "being managed" looks like, then I'm fine with being managed every day. As much as I want to see Jonathan, this is almost better.

Almost.

I look over at Christopher, curious if he feels the same. His gaze is out toward the horizon, his face calm and peaceful. The lines around his eyes are gone and his stern mouth is actually almost a smile. He looks happier than I've seen him in a long time. In all his business photos and the few times I've seen him around the house since taking over the company, he's always been serious and grim.

But right now, with the sun on his face and the sea air in his hair, he looks happy and carefree. It's a good look on him.

"When's the last time you took a vacation, Christopher?" I ask him.

"I don't know." He looks thoughtful for a moment. "I guess I took a day off in Tokyo last year."

"And?" I ask, thinking that a year ago is far too long to go without a break.

"I ate sushi." He shrugs. "To be honest, I don't really remember much of it. The jet lag was pretty rough."

That hardly sounds like a vacation to me.

"Did you see any of those fun vending machines? The ones with crazy things inside them?" I ask, thinking of all the things I want to see when I go to Tokyo someday. "Or go to one of those animal cafes? I heard about one that has owls and another that has hedgehogs."

Christopher shakes his head. "No. There's a cafe with hedgehogs? That seems like a health code violation."

"What did you do there then? I mean, other than eat sushi?"

Christopher frowns, thinking. "Business." He sips at his drink and glances over at me, the frown still darkening his face. "I guess it wasn't really a vacation."

Suddenly, he looks tired and worn. He has for a long time, I realize. He hides the stress behind tailored business suits, but the toll shows in other ways. There's a hint of silver in his dark hair that his brother doesn't have. There's lines around his mouth and eyes from glaring at underlings and reading contracts.

"Why do you do it?" I ask him, sipping on my own drink.

"What do you mean?" he asks. "Eat sushi? Because it's really tasty."

I chuckle and shake my head. "I mean, why do you work so hard?"

He squints out at the horizon and sighs. "I don't know. I just do. What else should I do except work?"

"Have fun?"

He scoffs. "Fun doesn't matter."

"I learned from working in the islands that play is just as important as work. Everything moves on island time here because you have to stop and appreciate the beauty around you," I tell him. There are other reasons for island time, but this is a good one. "You should enjoy life. Business will be there in the morning."

Christopher looks around, taking in the clear waters and darkening sky. The sun is lower now, nearly to touching the horizon. Everything is bathed in a warm red light that sparkles and dances on the tips of the waves.

"In a place like this, I can see why life might move slower," he says. "But that's not my life. I like being busy. I have to be busy."

"But why?" I press him. "You're already a billionaire. You have more money than you could ever spend, yet you can't remember the last time you enjoyed the fruits of that labor. Why do that to yourself?"

Christopher looks down at his drink. "I'm not nearly drunk enough to answer these kind of questions, Nora."

"Sorry," I say, realizing I might be pushing too hard.

"No, it's okay." He chugs the rest of his drink and smiles at me. He looks out at the ocean, his face full of thought. I give him a moment and finally he answers. His voice is soft and low, and I nearly miss hearing his words over the sound of the water.

"I think it's because I'm not sure what else to do."

"What do you mean?" I ask, not understanding how a billionaire with a solid future wouldn't know what to do with his life.

"I've been groomed to be the head of the company since I was born. There was never a question of what school I would go to, what I would major in, what job I would have, where I would live, or what I would do with my life," he explains. "It's always been to work. I suppose it's all I know how to do. It's the only thing I'm good at."

My heart squeezes with the honesty of his words. I bump my shoulder against his. "I don't know if it's the only thing you're good at," I tell him. "You're doing an excellent job of managing me. And no one sits on a dock with me as well as you."

He laughs, but there is a bitterness to it that taints the sound. "Now you're just being nice."

"No." I realize that I mean it. That there is more to this conversation than I first thought. I set my empty drink glass off to the side. "I started out today being annoyed with you. I've wanted to be with Jonathan since boys stopped having cooties, and you were taking away my chance."

"It's just business," he tells me, looking out at the ocean.

I shift so that I'm facing him with one leg up on the dock and the other hanging into the water. He is staring at the bare ice cubes in his glass and frowning. The setting sun washes everything in a warm orange light, yet his eyes are still marvelously blue. They capture the warm light and reflect it back at me.

"But this has been better than I expected," I tell him. "Much better." My heart pounds as I reach out and touch his shoulder. His skin is warm with the sun. "Thank you for managing me."

Christopher turns, his blue eyes dark and sad as he looks over me. There is a hint of a bitter smile on his face. "Oh, Nora." His voice is soft and bittersweet.

My hand goes from his shoulder to his cheek. The scruff of a day without shaving is rough against the palm of my hand. He has a five-o'clock shadow that I've never seen on him before. He's usually so rigid about staying clean-shaven that I'm not sure he's ever had a full beard. I like the scruff. It adds something to his face that makes my body heat. It's masculine and primal.

I swallow hard as time slows. My heart beats heavy in my chest. The sun hangs impossibly suspended over the ocean, casting the world in an endless golden light. Casting Christopher in golden light.

He's so much more than I've given him credit for. There's a connection between us. My hand feels right touching him, cementing that bond. His eyes go to mine, blue and deep as the ocean.

I don't think.

I lean forward, bringing my lips to his, and I kiss Christopher.

CHAPTER 14

The kiss is simple and sweet. Just our lips pressing together like they were meant to be that way. I like the way his lips feel against mine and tremble at the idea of more.

I pull back, my eyes searching his face. My hand is still on his cheek.

What am I doing? I ask myself. *Does he feel this connection too? Or is this all just in my head? Was this day as magical as I think it was, or is Christopher just that skilled in keeping me busy?*

All I know, is that right now, I want to kiss him. I want to do more than just kiss him.

Time resumes and the sun slips beneath the waves behind us, shadows growing longer with every passing second. My hand trembles as I wait for his reaction.

"Nora," he whispers. His pupils dilate, nearly swallowing up the blue of his eyes.

His hand is suddenly on the back of my head, pulling me into a new kiss. This new kiss is better than the last.

There is passion and desire in this kiss, a need that threatens to overwhelm both of us. This kiss is a little piece of heaven. His tongue finds mine, sweet with tequila.

Christopher is a good kisser. Perhaps the best kisser I've ever met. Somehow, this surprises and doesn't surprise me at the same time. He always had to be the best at everything, why would kissing be any different?

He pulls me to him, and I move, straddling his lap. His feet dangle into the ocean as my knees find their spot on either side of his hips. I fit in his lap like I was made to be here. I love the way his hands tangle in my hair, the way his arms wrap around me, the way his body responds to mine.

It feels right.

I gasp for breath, pulling back slightly and panting. The sun is gone and the warm night has taken over. Stars twinkle and the moon shines on the ocean, but all I can see is Christopher. All I want is more of him. His kisses are better than tequila at making me want more.

"Do we have this place for just the day, or did you rent it for the night as well?" I ask.

The corners of his mouth twitch upward and curl into a cocky smile. "All night."

I grin, my body heating at the idea of a night spent with kisses like these.

I don't have to say a word, I just slide from his lap and stand. He's standing in an instant, taking my hand and guiding me across the deck and back toward the room. The only sound is my heartbeat, his breathing, and the song of the ocean.

I pause at the doorway, suddenly unsure.

I love Jonathan, don't I? I ask myself. Here I am, about

to be with his brother while he is back home, helping his mother and missing me.

But is he missing me? I have to admit, most of our relationship was entirely in my head. He is also supposed to be getting engaged soon. He's not really mine to want.

"Nora?" Christopher stands in the doorway, sensing my thoughts. There's a hint of worry in his smile as he holds out a hand for me. I look him over, seeing him in a new light.

He's handsome in the twilight. His brown hair is messy with sun and wind, his eyes bright, and body strong. The tops of his shoulders are pink from the sun, and so is his nose.

He's not Jonathan.

He's Christopher.

He's the one who had dance lessons with me. He's the one that recognized me when I came home. He's the one that saved me from that party all those years ago. He's the brother that remembers me. He's the one that wanted me to be warm.

I've loved the wrong brother all these years. Jonathan is showy and fun, but he doesn't know me from the blonde walking down the street.

"Nora?" Christopher asks again.

I wonder how many times he's been passed over by a woman for his little brother.

I'm not sure I'm doing the right thing. I still have feelings for Jonathan, but I'm not sure they're real. Christopher, however, is real. He's waiting for me now.

Did I want to run away from Christopher? Did I want to stop what we were doing?

No. Stopping is the last thing I want to do. I want to

run to him, throw my arms around his neck and kiss him like crazy. I don't want to run anywhere but to Christopher.

It might be the tequila, or too much sun. It might be the wonderful conversation, or the feeling of being listened to. It might be nothing more than a fling.

It doesn't really matter why I want to be with Christopher tonight. Just that I want him.

I smile and take his hand.

The room is cool and I shiver slightly as I come inside. The night is dark all around us.

Christopher turns to me. "Are you sure?"

I smile at him and nod. "I am."

The smile that lights up his face casts any doubts away. Christopher pulls me into his arms and kisses me.

He tastes like tequila and fresh mangoes. I can't imagine anything tasting sweeter or more delicious. The scruff from his five-o'clock shadow rubs my skin, heightening every movement of his kisses. I crave them more than I crave oxygen.

I shrug out of my robe, letting it fall to the floor. He does the same. I'm not cold here. The room is still warm from the Caribbean sun.

I lick my lips, looking him over. The moon shines through the windows and gleams off the gentle curves of his muscles. There's butterflies in my stomach and heat coursing through my veins.

I've been with men before. I've had serious relationships and some not so serious ones. Sex isn't a mystery to me. Yet, looking him over, I want him more than I've ever wanted anyone. I want to lick the lines of his abs. I want to feel his fingers on my skin. I want to know exactly how he feels inside of me because I know, deep in my bones, that it will feel even better than I can imagine.

"You're so beautiful," he whispers. I was so busy looking him over that I didn't realize he was doing the same to me.

I kiss him again, feeling the heat of his skin press against mine. His fingers find the hook on the back of my bikini top and undo it. He unties the strap around my neck and pulls the fabric away from my body.

I shiver with desire as my bare breasts press against his chest. He's so warm and hard in all the right places. I want more. I want all of him to touch me everywhere. I couldn't get enough of him.

Christopher tips his head, kissing past my lips and to my neck, just below my earlobe. He nibbles and nips, kissing my skin and filling me with anticipation.

I can't stop the moan that escapes my lips. It's soft, but full of need. Christopher raises his head and grins at me, cocky and pleased with himself. He tugs me gently to the bed where we both can sit. I shimmy out of my swimsuit bottoms while he sits on the edge of the bed.

Christopher gives me a wicked grin, his eyes going up and down my body. It's a different smile than I've ever seen on him. I've seen the businessman smile, I've seen the happy smile, I've seen the smile that makes me go weak in the knees, but this is one that heats my spine to melting. It's sexy and hot and makes me want to jump onto the bed and have my way with him.

Which is my plan, but no need to rush things.

He beckons me to him and I step between his knees. His hands rest on my hips as he looks up at me with blue eyes full of desire. With my hands resting on top of

Christopher's broad shoulders, I pull myself close to him, pressing my chest against his face. The stubble on his cheeks tickles the sensitive skin and I can't help but moan again.

He brings his hands to my breasts, cupping each one like a delicate treasure. His pupils dilate as he carefully licks one nipple and then the other. He wraps his lips over the sensitive nub and begins to flick his tongue in a quick rhythm.

I close my eyes and focus on the wonderful sensations running through me. His fingers caress my bare skin as his mouth pleasures me. My knees are shaking with desire and pleasure. I put my knees up on either side of his waist, more to keep from falling over than anything.

Christopher groans slightly, his hands sliding down from my breasts, over the curve of my hips and feeling the swell of my butt. The obvious bulge in his swim trunks twitches beneath me, creating a fresh wave of heat.

My fingers go to the strings on his swim trunks. Slowly, I find the knot and work it free. He moves from side to side, twisting out of the fabric without taking me off of him. I can feel the length of his excitement press against me.

Our eyes meet.

If I was unsure, I'm not now. Not while I'm gazing into his eyes. They are deep and full of desire. There's a heat in their blue depths that stirs something in my soul, something I didn't even know was there. It's primal and suddenly I'm panting.

"Christopher," I pant. I didn't expect to feel this level of need so quickly.

"Not yet," he whispers, his hands going to my hips. He

uses his strength to flip me onto the bed so that I'm now beneath him, my legs wrapped around his waist. He gives me a naughty grin and then slides down.

He kisses the bare skin of my breasts, trailing kisses to my stomach. He keeps going, his kisses soft and teasing. Goosebumps form on my skin that have nothing to do with the temperature. He kisses the top of each thigh before kissing where they meet.

An explosion of sensation rushes through me, causing me to arch my back and spread my legs. Christopher makes a pleased sound and focuses his attention completely on making me moan.

He licks and teases, his fingers coming to help explore. Every time I whimper with pleasure, he does the motion again. My hands go to his head, my fingers tangling in his short hair. My legs start to shake as he flicks his tongue just a little bit faster. His fingers tease me with what's to come next.

Fireworks explode in my mind as he brings me to orgasm. It hardly took any time. It's like he knows what I need before I do. It's like he's in my head and knows what my body needs before I do. I've never come this quickly.

I go limp for a moment, my muscles twitching as the pleasure vibrates through every muscle in my body. Christopher looks up at me, that cocky grin filling his face. He looks pleased with himself.

"Christopher," I whimper, my eyelids still fluttering with the last bits of orgasm.

"I don't have a condom," he admits.

This is the last thing I want to hear. My head comes up and the good feelings eek away.

"What?"

"This wasn't exactly the plan," he admits.

I frown at him. "Wait, Christopher Lewis isn't prepared for something?" I shake my head at him. "That's a first."

An idea comes to me. I sit up and move to the nightstand. I pull open one of the drawers and grin as I find what I'm looking for: a full box of condoms. I hold one up triumphantly.

"Oh good," Christopher says with a grin. His head cocks to the side. "How did you know they would be there?"

"Jonathan." That's all I really need to say. This is where Jonathan brings his romantic dates. He wouldn't want to be stuck calling the concierge to bring condoms either. Since his secretary set everything up the way Jonathan would have it, I just looked where Jonathan would want them.

Christopher takes the condom from me with a smile. "I never thought I'd thank my little brother for this," he tells me, carefully opening the package.

I watch with lustful eyes as he puts the condom on. I want every inch of him like I've never wanted anyone before. There's something about him that my body craves, something that I don't think I'll ever get enough of.

I'm sitting on my knees, my eyes glued to his perfect body. Now it's my turn to beckon him to me. He crawls up onto the bed and kisses me, slowly wrapping his arms around me and lowering me onto the sheets.

He touches my cheek before sliding into me. The moment we join, a soft hiss escapes my lips. It's pure pleasure, pure desire, and complete relaxation. He feels so right with me, like this is where he should always have been.

Our hips rise and fall in tandem as we create love. The muscles in his chest and torso flex and relax with each pump. My own hips writhe and undulate to greet him, wanting more of him with every thrust. Every time he pulls back, I ache to have him fill me again, yet once he's deep I never want to let him go.

I am the only focus of his attention. His lips, hands, and body all are tuned to my pleasure, and my body to his. We move in tandem, our bodies following a dance that we never had to practice. There is an eagerness to his movements, a desire to please. It doesn't match with the cold hearted billionaire everyone claims he is. It matches with the man I just spent the evening talking and laughing with, though.

His breathing comes fast and hard. Mine matches as I gasp for air and yet don't want to stop. Every nerve in my body is screaming for him. Needing him to find completion and knowing that when he does, I will too. I know it as sure as I know my name. There is no way that he won't send me over the edge.

"Nora," he groans, his eyes coming to mine. There's a beautiful softness to them that heats my heart. His pace increases, a primal energy coming over him. He felt good before, but this makes that look tame.

This is pure, primal desire. I feel wanted in a way that I've never felt before. I want to feel him explode within me. I need to feel it. My body matches his, thrust for thrust. Every muscle in my body is primed to accept him, to take him ever deeper into me.

He groans and his breath quickens. His eyes meet mine and then go wide.

The knowledge that I did this to him is powerful. My

own body follows his to ecstasy, shivering and quaking as we find release in one another. Colors swirl and twist as every nerve in my body explodes because of Christopher.

He groans, tucking his head into my shoulder. We're both breathing hard and I know that I couldn't stand right now if I wanted to. I don't want to move. I love the weight of him on top of me. He feels so right. This feels so right.

He raises his head, a dazed smile crossing his face and I know this was meant to be.

My only thoughts are of Christopher. I can't think of anything but his smile and how good he feels inside of me. Of how much I don't want this moment to end. This is a heaven I didn't even know existed, yet now I know that I don't want to live without it.

He rolls to the side, his muscular chest still panting with exertion.

I kiss his cheek and then snuggle into his shoulder.

"That was good," I tell him, even though that's the understatement of the year.

"Just good?" He frowns at me. I grin.

"Better than good. Great," I amend. I can't seem to think of any longer words. My brain is still too fried on orgasm.

"I can do better than great," he tells me, that cocky smile coming back. My heart speeds up, even though it never really had the chance to slow down.

"Again?" I look down and see he's already recovering.

He just grins and kisses me.

CHAPTER 15

The sound of Christopher's voice wakes me.

The dawn is coming, but it's still dark outside. The sound of the ocean against the pillars below us remains steady. There are no birds or animals moving yet. It's still dark, with just the gray image of light soon to come.

I sit up in bed, unsure of where I am. I look around, getting my bearings. The bed next to me is empty and cool to the touch. I'm not sure how long Christopher has been gone. I look around, trying to figure out what woke me.

I hear Christopher in the next room. Yellow light gleams from under the door. It's bright and artificial looking against the gray of dawn in the bedroom.

"No, the merger takes precedence. I don't care what it costs, get their lawyers in line. This is going forward as planned." Christopher's voice is frustrated.

I slide out of bed, the sheets hissing as I move. The floor is cool on my bare feet and I grab my robe from where I tossed it the night before. I wrap it around me, surprised that I'm still naked. I never sleep naked. I like the security of pajamas, but last night, I'd been safe in Christopher's arms.

I creep over to the door, listening to the conversation. I can only hear one side of it as Christopher is on his phone. Given the frustration in Christopher's voice, I know it's about the merger. Christopher has a lot of money on the line, not to mention personal pride. It isn't hard to imagine why he'd be stressed about things going poorly.

I put my hand on the doorknob, planning on going in and saying good morning. Maybe I might even be able to convince Christopher to leave his phone long enough to come back to bed before the sun rises.

"Yes, yes. Jonathan is still going to propose to Adeline. You don't have to worry about the woman from the restaurant," Christopher says. The door is still closed but I can imagine him pacing the room. I don't want to interrupt, so I pause, not opening the door. "Of course I'm taking care of things... I'm doing whatever it takes. Jonathan won't be compromised."

Whatever it takes...

The words hit me like tiny daggers and I remember the reason I'm here. This isn't a romantic holiday. This is a distraction. This is to keep me away from Jonathan. What happened last night was wonderful, but it still accomplished Christopher's first mission: keep me away from Jonathan.

I thought Christopher and I had shared something special last night, but now, I'm not so sure. Maybe he really was just doing whatever it took to keep me out of the arms of his brother. Maybe I'm not as wanted as I thought.

My hand comes off the doorknob like it burned me. I shouldn't have been eavesdropping, but that doesn't change the hurt bubbling up inside of my chest. There is a very real possibility that Christopher isn't really interested in me and just took an easy opportunity for some fun. I silently move away from the door and go out to the porch. I don't want to hear any more of his conversation.

I might hear something that would really make me regret my choice last night. I know that last night was more about the physical than the emotional. I accept that. Christopher doesn't get involved with women, and there is no reason why I would be any different than any other woman in his life.

I know this, yet the idea that I'd been used still hurt more than I could have expected.

I push the thoughts away and look out at the lagoon. Dawn is creeping across the water on the waves. The world is still painted in dark blues and grays, matching my current mood. Soon though, the sun will come up over the island and turn the water into the brilliant Caribbean blue that I love. Perhaps with the dawn, I, too, will feel brighter.

I pick up the white telephone and order breakfast. There's a small coffee pot and different kinds of gourmet packets of coffee in the bar. I make a pot and then curl up in one of the chairs to sip my drink and watch the water grow bright. Breakfast arrives in minutes and is quickly set up on the table. The servers are gone almost too fast for me to thank them.

Slowly, the lagoon comes to life. The skies turn from gray to pink to crystal blue. The water brightens from dark to brilliant. The sun shines and the world goes on. I feel a peace that only the ocean can bring wash over me. I am small against the ocean. My problems are small against the ocean.

I take my coffee and sit on the edge of the dock, my feet in the water. We sat here last night, but it feels like a different world today. I'm not sure what to think of Christopher today. What I overheard changes things. I like him, but I don't know how he feels about me. I don't know if this was all just an elaborate charade to keep me busy or if he likes me the way I like him.

It's probably best if I keep my heart closed, I decide. I can enjoy what we have, but I can't and won't let myself fall for him. Better to keep this a friends with benefits arrangement than have my heart broken.

Loving Christopher is asking for a broken heart.

I hear the door behind me open and shut. Christopher is emerging from his phone calls and work. I turn and smile at him, determined to be pleasant.

"There's coffee in the pot," I tell him. "And I ordered a little bit of everything for breakfast. I wasn't sure if you preferred sweet or savory."

"Thanks." He pours himself a cup of coffee and looks over the food. He chooses a couple of slices of bacon and some fresh fruit.

He's wearing slacks and a polo. It's still incredibly dressed down for him, but very overdressed for the Caribbean. Especially since I'm still naked under my robe.

"The hotel gets five stars from me," I tell him. "They've done everything I can think of to make this a high class experience. As long as you get to keep the staff, I think you'll have a great resort purchase."

"Other than not having a blender," he replies, flashing me a small grin.

"Except the blender," I agree with a chuckle. I sip at my coffee. "How's business?"

"Fine." He picks out another piece of fruit for his plate. "Our flight leaves in an hour."

"Oh." I look out at the water, feeling homesick for this place already.

"Uh, I guess we could stay here if you want," he tells me, but his body language says otherwise. He looks incredibly uncomfortable with the idea of being away from his business. The tension in his muscles makes him look like he might bolt for the door at the first chance. He hasn't even sat down yet to eat.

"No, it's fine." I shake my head. "I think you might wither away and die if you stay away from your office for too long."

"Ha ha." He rolls his eyes and takes sip of coffee. He's drinking it black. There is no room for sweetness or comfort in his world.

"Come sit with me." I pat the bare wood next to me.

He hesitates, a frown crossing his face. His hand automatically reaches toward his phone. "I don't know..."

"Are things going to change that much in the next hour? You can have the whole plane ride back to work. You don't get to sit and watch the sunrise over the ocean every day."

He stiffens for a moment, but then carries his plate and coffee mug to sit by me. He doesn't put his feet in the water since he's wearing slacks and already has his shoes and socks on. Instead, he pulls over one of the chairs and sits in it instead.

"There. That wasn't so hard," I tell him. He gives me

an annoyed side eye and pops a piece of fruit into his mouth.

His face suddenly brightens and he points out across the water. "Look, the dolphins are back." The stiff posture disappears and he's smiling as he watches the dolphins dance around the lagoon. I watch him for a moment. He looks happy. Calm. I see the man I made love to last night as he smiles at the water.

His phone chirps and it all disappears. Gone is the man who smiles and points out the fish. His mouth thins and the light in his eyes fades. He stops eating and pulls out his phone. He types something and puts the phone away, but the grim face remains.

"I'm going to have another cup of coffee," I say, rising to my feet. "Do you need more?"

He shakes his head. I go and refill my cup, and when I come back I find that he's placed a chair next to him on the deck. There isn't much space, so the chairs are touching. I smile and settle into the chair, leaning back and watching the water as we both sip our coffees.

Christopher puts his arm on the back of my chair. The motion is awkward, like a high school boy trying to sneak an arm around a date, but I like it anyway. I rest my head on his shoulder. For a brief moment, he stiffens, but then relaxes. He lets his arm wrap around me and I can see him smile out of the corner of my eye.

The heat of the tropics rises quickly with the sun. The water looses its morning paleness and turns to blue crystal. Below us, the fish swirl and glitter. I wish that we could stay here in this moment, but I know soon the heat will be too much. Besides, we have a plane to catch. We have to go back to the real world.

Christopher's phone starts to ring. He tenses. I can tell he's using every fiber of his being to resist answering the phone and ruining the moment.

"Answer it," I tell him. "I should get ready anyway."

His arm is gone from around me and the phone to his ear in a second. The soft look vanishes from his face and he's back to the businessman yet again. I try not to sigh as I get up and head to the bungalow to gather my things.

Inside, I quickly dress and gather my few belongings. I wash my face and brush my hair. Christopher stays out on the porch, the phone glued to his ear.

I look around the room, taking in every detail. In the light of day, it looks different than it did last night. Less magical, more practical. It's still beautiful, but it lacks the sparkle that made last night dreamlike. I sigh.

Was it all a dream? Did I really feel a connection to him last night, or was it just the tequila and a beautiful setting? I'm not sure.

I'm not sure what I feel now. Even with the mind-blowing sex, I'm not sure exactly how to feel about Christopher. I like him. I like him a lot, but I'm not sure that the feeling is mutual. I'm afraid that the feelings will all fade as soon as we leave the bungalow. That we'll realize what we've done and regret it.

"Ready?" Christopher asks, walking in from the porch. His phone is still in his hand and he's wearing his serious face.

"Christopher..." I pause, unsure of how I want to phrase this. "What did last night mean?"

His eyes are serious. "We were two consenting adults enjoying a wonderful evening."

"And that's all?" I don't know what I want him to say

next. I'm terrified he's going to say that he loves me and equally afraid he's going to say it was a mistake.

"Nora, I don't do relationships." His mouth thins and there's no joy in his eyes.

"So, this was just business." I take a breath and nod. "I can handle that. I just want to make sure we're on the same page."

"Just business," he agrees. His voice softens. "And business can be fun sometimes."

"Last night was fun," I agree. "And I think you're right. Just two consenting adults enjoying this place. Nothing more."

"Good."

I linger for a moment longer, looking over the bungalow. I'm not sure how I feel about all this. Relieved, maybe? There isn't anything going on between Christopher and I, other than taking advantage of a good time. I don't have to complicate this with emotions. Christopher certainly hasn't.

He doesn't spare a second glance as we walk away. There is no longing backward look at the bungalow as we hurry along the boardwalk, through the lobby, and out to the waiting limo.

He's on his phone again the moment we enter the limo. I listen to him talk to other heads of departments about billing hours and transitional teams. I stare out the window and watch our island getaway disappear.

Maybe it was all just a dream.

We board the airplane and before I'm even done putting on my seat-belt, there is a fizzy lemonade in my hands. I sip at it. If nothing else, I learned I have a new favorite drink.

The plane takes off with Christopher still on his phone.

I sip at my drink and watch the window. I watch as the bright blue waters turn dark and we fly over the ocean. Soon, we'll hit the coast and fly up that way, but for now, we're over deep water. I imagine that whales are down there watching us fly over them, curious about the strange beings in the sky.

It takes me a moment to realize that Christopher is quiet. I look away from the window to see him staring out his window as well. His phone is in his lap without a current phone call, although it blinks with things to do.

I look in wonder at him stopping and enjoying the scenery. He is taking a moment to look at the world. It makes me smile and wonder what other surprises he might have in store.

CHAPTER 16

It's late afternoon when we get back to the mansion. The sun is hot and there isn't a cloud in the sky. It's smoggy in the city, but clear by the estate.

I step out of the limo and into the driveway. It feels different to be here now. This is where I've loved Jonathan all my life. To be here now feels like I've betrayed that memory somehow.

"Oh no." Guilt pulls on me with invisible strings, making me heavy.

"What?" Christopher asks. He slides his phone back into his pocket, but I can already hear it vibrating with some sort of urgent message. All Christopher's messages are urgent.

"I promised Jonathan I would call him," I reply. I wince, feeling shame and guilt roll through me. "I totally forgot."

I forgot to call him because I was too busy doing his brother.

"I wouldn't worry," Christopher advises me. "I'm pretty sure he was busy keeping my mother from freaking out. You were the least of his concerns."

For some reason, the comment stings a little more than I expect.

"I should call him," I say, looking toward the main house. "Do you think they're back yet?"

"Probably. Sure. Go for it. Check the house." Christopher gives me a fake smile and I now have a different kind of guilt pulling at me. If it's not one brother, it's the other.

I hurry over to the main house. It's cold inside with air conditioned drafts making me shiver as I head up the stairs to Jonathan's room. The house is quiet, but I can hear the TV on in Jonathan's room. The door is open.

I knock twice and peek my head in.

"Hey," a drowsy voice calls from the bed.

I step into the room, feeling a flutter of excitement go through me. I'm in Jonathan's room. This is a place of dreams for me.

Jonathan is on top of the sheets, still wearing shorts and a t-shirt. He has a cold washcloth draped over his eyes, but he's holding up one end to look at me.

"Hey." I walk over to the bed, feeling self conscious about where I should stand. This is his bedroom. Can I lean against the bed? Should I stay as far away as possible? Can I climb into bed with him?

"You have no idea the night I had," Jonathan tells me, putting the washcloth back over his eyes.

There's no way I'm telling him about my night.

"I heard you were at the hospital," I say. I've chosen to stay a respectable distance from the bed.

"Yeah. Come closer. I'm not going to bite," he tells me, a smile filling what I can see of his face. "In fact, come up here. It's easier to talk that way."

He scoots over, giving me a space on the bed. I stare at it for a moment and swallow hard. My steps are timid as I come closer and put my knee on the bed.

This is something I've dreamed of since boys stopped being gross. To be in bed with Jonathan is something I'm not really prepared for.

"Lay down," he tells me. "I'm afraid I'm not up for much more. I've got a wicked headache."

"I'm sorry," I tell him. "Can I do anything?"

"Unfortunately, no." He sighs. "I took some medicine and I'm hoping to pass out soon. I'm glad you stopped by though." He raises the washcloth and glares at me. "You're not laying down."

"Sorry." I wiggle next to him, putting my head on the pillow beside him. His body radiates warmth and he smells amazing. "So, the hospital?"

"Right. My mother was doing morning yoga with one of her friends, Lynn. Lynn started having horrible chest pain and mom was sure she was having a heart attack," he explains. "They took Lynn in an ambulance but Mom needed me to drive her to the hospital. Lynn doesn't have any family nearby and my mother was in no condition to drive."

"What about the chauffeur?" I ask. "Or my dad?"

"Mom wanted me there to help out," Jonathan answers. "It was a good thing too. I was fairly certain Mom was going to have a heart attack, too, the way she was acting. I spent the whole evening keeping her calm. Every time one of the machines would start beeping, they would both start acting like they were going to die."

"Is Lynn okay?" I ask, still feeling very strange about laying in bed with Jonathan.

"Yeah. Turns out it was just gas and stress," he says with a chuckle. "I'm sorry we weren't able to talk. I have some things I'd really like to discuss with you."

"Me too." Guilt tugs at me. I should not be in bed with him after being in bed with Christopher.

"But not right now," Jonathan murmurs. "I need to sleep. I've been up all night. The meds are finally kicking in. You can tell me your night later."

"Okay," I tell him. "You rest."

I watch as his breathing slows and evens. I watch him sleep for a few minutes, just laying in the dark next to him. He looks so peaceful, so content. I wonder if Christopher looks this way when he sleeps too. I didn't see him last night. I fell asleep before he did and he was gone when I woke up.

Thinking of Christopher makes me anxious to leave Jonathan's bed.

"Bye, Jonathan," I say softly, but there is no response.

I reach out and brush a lock of hair from his forehead. It's so much longer than Christopher's. I've always wondered what it would feel like to run my fingers through Jonathan's hair. It's softer than I thought it would be.

I smooth his hair one last time before standing. I leave him sleeping peacefully, the TV on low and a blanket draped over him.

At the door it hits me. I was just in bed with Jonathan. Granted, it wasn't really the way I thought it would be and was far more platonic than anything, but still. I should be excited, but all I feel is guilt.

I sigh and shake my head at myself as I close the door to his room. The Lewis brothers are going to destroy my emotional well-being.

"I have a favor to ask of you," Christopher says.

I squint up at him, the morning sunlight bright behind his head. I have a book in my hands as I sit on the bottom step to my dad's apartment, but I'm not really reading. My brain is more focused on Christopher and Jonathan than on the words on the page. I spent a restless night thinking about the two of them, and the book isn't helping me get my mind off of either of them.

I have years of wanting Jonathan on one side, and a night of passion on the other. How am I supposed to choose between them?

"What kind of favor?" I ask warily. I have a feeling that there is more to this request than just driving him to the airport or loaning him a cup of sugar.

"It's kind of a last-minute thing," he tells me. He sounds casual and unconcerned, but he's playing with his cuff links. It's another one of his tells. Cuticles and cuff links mean he's nervous.

Christopher is wearing his traditional suit. It's dark

gray today with a pale blue tie. His hair is neatly brushed back and the only indication of our trip is that his nose is still a little sunburned.

I tentatively lower my book. "What do you need?"

"A date."

My eyebrows rise in surprise. "A date?"

"I have a charity thing. It's in the city. It's fancy," he explains. He sounds calm, but his fingers twist his cuff links to the point where I'm afraid he's going to rip them out of his jacket. "I need someone to hang on my arm and look pretty. You're pretty, so I thought you could help me out."

"Wow, what a compliment," I tease him. "Such a charmer."

He almost smiles at me, his eyes crinkling just enough to let me know he finds me amusing. "So?"

"I don't have a dress," I tell him with a shrug.

"I can get you a dress."

Again, my eyebrows raise. "You'll get me a dress? I didn't know you knew fashion."

"Well, my secretary will get you one." His eyes crinkle at the corners again. "She has much better taste than I do."

I squint into the bright light behind him until he moves to the side. I wonder if he's hot in his suit. Physically warm, I mean. I know he looks attractive. Meanwhile, I'm chilly in my capri pants and t-shirt, even though the day is already warm. The humidity is high, but I still miss the Caribbean warmth.

"You're managing me again, aren't you?" I look up at him and sigh. It's not just him. Everyone on staff suddenly has things for me to do to keep me busy.

I know that they're worried about what Jonathan will

do. I know that despite what happened on our trip, Christopher will still worry about me seducing his brother. Given that Jonathan told me he loved me yesterday, Christopher is still worried about Jonathan really falling in love with me, or saying something inappropriate in front of the wrong people. They want him to marry Adeline and it's best to keep me from his sight. The less he sees of me, the less likely he is to do something rash.

It's not just me Christopher is managing. It's Jonathan, too. If I'm not here, Jonathan can't fall in love with me. He can't do something stupid with me if I'm not near him.

"You liked it well enough last time I managed you," Christopher replies. He gives his brows a little waggle and winks at me.

"Yes, I did." I blush a little remembering just how good a time I had with him. "I don't think you had such a bad time either."

A hint of a smile crosses his face, and he manages to make it look cocky and sexy. "You're right."

I think about my answer for a moment. Should I try to see Jonathan again, or should I just go with Christopher? I know that even if I say no, the Family will find ways to keep me busy. I might as well choose the enjoyable version of being managed. Besides, as much as it pains me to say it, I like spending time with Christopher.

"Okay. You can manage me," I tell him with a smile. It's better to go with the flow than try to fight the Lewis family when they have plans.

A real smile fills Christopher's face and my heart forgets how to beat for a moment. His smile is brighter than the sun and better than ice cream on a hot day. I don't think he expected me to say yes so easily.

"I'll pick you up at five," he tells me.

"And the dress?"

"You'll have it in an hour."

I narrow my eyes. "You had this planned. You already had a dress picked out."

"Maybe a little," he admits, still smiling. It's hard to be mad at him when he grins at me.

"What if I had said no?" I ask him, crossing my arms.

He shrugs. "There are backup plans. This one is the most fun, though."

I sigh and shake my head. "Always planning. Always one step ahead."

"That's how you win at business," he informs me.

"I suppose it is." I uncross my arms and pick my book back up. I lost a game I didn't even know I was playing. "I'll see you at five."

Christopher doesn't leave right away. He hesitates for just a moment before leaning over and kissing my cheek. It's just a small peck on the cheek, but it makes my pulse zoom and my girl parts heat. His kiss is electric.

He's gone before I can say anything. My hand goes to my cheek as I watch him confidently walk away. His strides are long and sure as he heads to his home office, and I'm enjoying the view of him walking away. His suits are very nicely tailored to show off his assets.

There's butterflies in my stomach as I try to find my place in my book once more. Yet again, I'm not paying any attention to the printed letters in front of me. I'm too excited thinking about tonight. If the vacation was good, what kind of things did Christopher have in store at home?

CHAPTER 18

The dress is magnificent.

Hunter green satin with a matching lace overlay falls from a boat neck cut that accentuates my collar bones. The bodice is tight without being restrictive and the skirt is long and tight, but with a slit up to my thigh. It's classy and sexy, and of course, it fits perfectly.

I wonder what Christopher told his secretary to get the measurements so correct.

"You look lovely," Dad says, walking into the living room. It's almost five and I'm trying to wait patiently by the door without actually looking like I'm waiting. Despite wearing an evening gown, I've tidied up the living room and unloaded the dishwasher. If I wasn't afraid of splashing water on my dress, I'd do the dishes in the sink and scrub it too.

"Thank you," I tell my dad, smiling at the compliment.

"Here, let me fix your hair." Dad comes over and carefully smooths a strand of hair away from my face. He smiles as he steps back and looks me over. "You've grown so much. Your mother would be so proud of you."

This means more to me than any compliment on my appearance he could give. "Thank you, Dad."

"Who would have thought my little girl would be going to a charity dinner with the Lewis family?" He shakes his head gently. I haven't told him everything, but my dad is a smart man and the maids gossip. I'm sure he knows that Jonathan is interested in me and that I had an overnight trip with Christopher. "You must be going with Mrs. Lewis since Jonathan still isn't feeling well."

"I'm not going with Mrs. Lewis," I tell him. "I'm going with Christopher."

Dad doesn't hide his unhappy surprise well. "Oh. Christopher. Again?"

"He's just keeping me away from Jonathan. He'll do anything to keep the merger going, even if it means taking me out on the town."

Dad narrows his eyes. "I think it's more than that."

I haven't told Dad anything about our trip. Just that we stayed in the Caribbean and it was work related. But he's not stupid.

"It's nothing, Dad," I assure him, even though I'm not so sure myself.

"I don't know," Dad says, his eyes unhappy as he looks me over again. His eyes linger on the slit of my dress. It's perfectly respectable, but I feel like I should hide it. "I think Christopher may finally be making a move."

I try not to roll my eyes. "Christopher isn't in high school and making moves on girls," I tell him. "Besides, I'm not his type."

"He has liked you for a long time. Ever since that time

you came home from college and stayed here a week. He couldn't stop staring at you," Dad informs me.

"What?" I wonder if I should get my dad screened for dementia.

"A father notices. You were too busy staring at Jonathan to see Christopher staring at you," Dad tells me.

"No," I reply, shaking my head. "Why would he have any interest in me? I'm the butler's daughter. He only knows me because he caught me swimming in his pool once."

"He let you keep swimming if I recall," Dad says, crossing his arms.

"That's not the point," I tell him. "You really don't have to worry about Christopher. He's all business. You know that."

"I suppose you're right." Dad kisses my cheek. " Have fun tonight. Be careful, though. Jonathan is a playboy and might break your heart, but he doesn't do it out of malice. To be honest, I would worry about you less with him. I know what Jonathan wants."

"And what does Christopher want?" I ask. "We both know it's just money."

"I'm not exactly sure with Christopher, but I don't trust him," Dad says. "I do know that for Christopher, business always comes first. I've seen him do some questionable things in the name of making money."

"Well, it's a good thing I have no money then," I tell him. Still, I wonder what Christopher is doing with me as well. Is this all for the merger money, or does he feel something for me? I know I need to guard my heart against him. Christopher's even said as much.

Dad doesn't think my pithy answer is very funny and

he frowns at me. Luckily, the doorbell rings and I don't have to have this conversation anymore.

"Don't worry about me, Dad." I give him a hug. "I love you."

"I love you too, Kiddo," he replies. He sneaks one more kiss on my cheek, which I happily receive.

I hurry over and open the door to find Christopher standing on the porch. He looks amazing in his tuxedo, like something out of a fashion magazine. He kept his hair simple and neat, and he's clean shaven. I almost wish there were scruff though. I liked the scruff.

"Christopher." My dad gives Christopher a stern look. It's the look men give their daughter's dates when they want the boy to know who is in charge. I half expect that I'll come home to find my father cleaning a shotgun on the porch.

"Good evening, Mr. Bailey," Christopher replies. He's cool as a cucumber and completely unfazed by my father. I suppose he's faced down angry board members and investors scarier than my father.

"You two behave yourselves," Dad says as I walk out the door. He gives another stern look at Christopher. "You be good, Christopher."

"Of course, sir," Christopher replies with a polite head nod.

I wave to my dad and close the door behind me. The sun is still up and everything is warm with golden light. The hum of insects fills the air as the frogs and crickets haven't come out to play yet.

The limo is waiting for us at the bottom of the stairs. One benefit of living over the garage is that the walk to the car isn't very far. The interior of the limo is cool as I slide across the leather. I'm getting used to riding in limos, which seems very strange to me.

Christopher follows me in. He carefully puts his phone in his breast pocket and takes the seat across from me.

"What is this a fundraiser for?" I ask as the car begins to move.

"I'm actually not sure," he replies with a shrug. "Maybe a hospital?"

"You were that desperate to get me away from the house that you don't even know what we're doing?" I ask, crossing my arms.

"No, I was that excited to have an excuse to see you again," he replies.

I can't help but to smile at that. "Nice recovery," I tell him.

He grins at me. "I know my audience."

I shake my head at him, but there's still a flutter of butterflies in my stomach.

"So, how was your day?" I ask him. I expect he'll pull out his phone at any moment and start doing business, but I feel like we should at least attempt to have a conversation.

"It was good," he replies. "There's a few complications with the merger, but overall things are going smoothly. As long as things stay the way they are now, I'll be a happy camper. How about you? Do you like the dress?"

"I do," I tell him.

"What were you reading earlier?" he asks. "When I asked you to come with me this morning."

"Um, it's a book on hotel management," I reply. "It's fairly technical, but a good analysis on retaining quality employees."

"Tell me more."

I sit there with my mouth open for a moment, unsure of where to start. I'm expecting him to pull out his phone, but he hasn't yet. If anything, he's paying complete attention to me. It's a heady feeling to have Christopher Lewis's full attention.

I start to tell him about the book and we have a conversation of the cost benefit ratios of training new employees versus retaining old ones. It's a great conversation, and given that he owns a business, not terribly surprising that he knows a lot about it. What is surprising is that he isn't working. He's focusing solely on me and our conversation.

I barely notice when the limo pulls to a stop. We've talked the entire way into the city and to the hotel with the fund raising gala. Not once did he pull out his phone or attempt to do any work.

A girl could think she was important when a man did that.

"Thank you for doing this," Christopher says as the limo door opens. He steps out and offers me his hand. "You look amazing."

"Thank you." I take his hand, feeling his warmth run through my skin. I stand from the limo and take a look around.

It's my first time on a red carpet. There are photographers and beautiful people everywhere. I see security and there are even velvet ropes keeping those not invited out of the event.

I flash a grin to Christopher and take a step onto the red carpet. Except, I trip on my dress and immediately start to face plant.

What a way to walk a red carpet.

CHAPTER 19

"Whoa, there," Christopher says, catching my arm and keeping me upright. "You haven't even had anything to drink yet."

My hand goes to my chest, my palm shaking against my skin. The sudden rush of adrenaline has me trembling, and it's combining with the adrenaline of walking a red carpet. I take a shaky breath.

"You okay?" Christopher asks. He still has his hand on me, keeping me from tipping over. I'm glad, because I feel like I might fall without him there.

"Just embarrassed," I tell him. I give him a unsteady smile. "What a way to make an entrance, right?"

"Don't worry. No one saw a thing," he assures me. He moves my hand to his elbow. I remember practicing walking with him like this when we were younger. Learning how to properly escort a lady into a dance was part of his dance lessons.

The hotel is grand. The party is lavish, and the guests are all rich. There are senators and movie stars mingling with drinks in their hands. I swallow hard. I've seen this world from the outside, but never with the chance to enter. I'm glad Christopher is here to be my guide.

"Christopher? What are you doing here?" Deborah asks, gracefully crossing the room to greet us.

She's wearing a beautiful maroon satin gown. She's decided to embrace her age, and her gray hair is carefully piled on top of her head. Silver jewelry accents the silver of her hair. Her blue eyes match those of her children.

"Mother, it's good to see you." Christopher kisses her cheek. "You remember Nora?"

"Nora?" Deborah frowns and looks me over. She can't seem to place me and then her eyes go wide. "Nora Bailey? The butler's daughter? *That* Nora?"

I try not to react with anything but a polite smile. It's hard because I can feel the heat rising in my cheeks. "Hello, Mrs. Lewis. It's a pleasure to see you here."

"Good lord, child. I didn't recognize you at all," Deborah tells me. She looks me over, her eyes going up and down my dress. Yet again, the slit in the skirt feels provocative and like there are neon arrows pointing to it.

"Do you mind if I speak to my mother for a moment?" Christopher asks, pulling his mom off to the side.

I nod and take a step back. Christopher is whispering something in her ear. She looks surprised and then frowns. She looks at Christopher, her face stern and says something I can't hear.

I know they are talking about me. I know that they are talking about Jonathan. I know what the conversation is about, even if I can't hear it.

A waiter passes by and I take a glass of champagne. It's a struggle not to simply chug it.

"Sorry about that," Christopher says, coming back to me.

"You look lovely, dear," Deborah tells me. "I'm glad you're sitting at our table."

She gives me a polite smile and then turns to greet other party goers. I take another drink of champagne and wonder if this really was the best option. Maybe we could have gone to Martha's Vineyard this time. The rain doesn't sound so bad. I finish my champagne and give it to a waiter. I look around for a fresh glass, but don't see one.

"Dance with me," Christopher says. It's not really a request, but not quite a command. He holds out his hand to me and gives me a small smile. I can hear music in the ballroom.

"You're just trying to make sure I have a good time," I tell him, taking his hand. "I hope you're a better dancer than you used to be."

The ballroom floor is scattered with various couples dancing. Most of them are older than Christopher and I, and I look around trying not to feel self-conscious and failing.

"Don't worry about them," Christopher whispers to me, pulling me into his arms. His hand is steady and warm on my waist. His grip on my hand is confident. "Just dance with me."

We start to dance, swaying and stepping to the music. The last time we danced I was twelve and Christopher needed someone to practice his dancing lessons with. He'd stepped on my toes more times than I care to remember.

Christopher leads me through the dance, his hand pushing and pulling with just enough strength to tell me he is in charge. I follow his lead easily as he guides me through the motions of the dance. I can't help but smile as he spins me around, my skirt flaring out like a princess in a movie.

He pulls me into him, keeping me close as the song slows and comes to an end. With every breath, I can smell him. He still smells of sunshine and warmth. I breath in the scent of him, closing my eyes and focusing on the way he feels next to me.

He feels right. Like this is where I'm supposed to be. That only makes my brain more confused about what my heart wants. Do I want Christopher? I'm fairly sure I do, but I don't dare to love him at the same time.

There's a smattering of applause for the musicians as the song comes to an end. I smile up at Christopher and see him smile back down at me.

"See? I remembered," he tells me. There's a soft smile on his face that makes my heart speed up. "I didn't even step on your feet once."

I giggle, feeling lighter now. This dance was different than before. Despite the fact that there are far more people here, this dance feels more intimate than the one in the pool house. Maybe it's just that I know him better now. Maybe it's that there is more of a connection between us. Dancing is more fun when you know your partner.

"Christopher? Is that you?" a female voice asks.

Christopher loses the soft smile and his eyes dim. I turn and see a couple coming to greet him. The woman is probably around my age, but with enough plastic surgery that she's no longer biodegradable. There's a man with her, paunchy and ruddy, but wearing an expensive tux. The ring on the woman's finger looks big enough to buy a small nation.

"Sarabeth," Christopher greets the woman. "And Donald. How nice to see you."

"We never see you at these things, Christopher," Sarabeth gushes. She looks over at me, doing a head to toe examination. This time I don't feel bad about the slit. "And you even brought a date."

"Sarabeth, Donald, this is Nora. She's a friend of the family." I appreciate that he doesn't introduce me as the butler's daughter. A friend of the family sounds important and like I'm on equal footing.

"A pleasure to meet you," Sarabeth tells me. I'm fairly sure that she's sincere, but the upper part of her face isn't moving so it's hard to tell. She's smiling, but only her lips move. Her forehead and eyes are frozen in place.

"It's nice to meet you," I tell them.

"Christopher, do you have a moment?" Donald asks. He pulls Christopher off to the side. From the look on Christopher's face, it's clear that they're talking about the merger. It seems it's all anyone wants to talk about.

"Oh, it's so nice to see Christopher bring a date to one of these things," Sarabeth tells me. "He never comes to these fundraisers. Usually he just sends Jonathan and a check."

"He did say it was a rather last minute decision to come," I reply. I look over to Christopher. I want to go back to dancing with him.

"It's good to see him, especially with someone. We've all been wondering when he'll tie the knot or at least bring a date to a function twice." Sarabeth laughs like she's made a terribly clever joke. "Jonathan never seems to have that problem."

"For being brothers, they are definitely different," I tell

her. I try to take a step away, but Sarabeth just stays close to me.

"Speaking of brothers, you look like just his type," Sarabeth says. "Jonathan's, I mean. I don't know what type Christopher has. Green and rich, I suppose. Add a couple of dollar signs to your dress and you're perfect for him."

I take a step away from the woman. She's not entirely wrong about Christopher, but I don't like her speaking about him like that.

"Christopher is a great guy," I tell her.

She looks me up and down and chuckles. "Sure. It helps that he's rich."

I hate the insinuation that I'm only after his money. Righteous indignation wells up inside of me. I wish I had a clever comeback or a witty retort to throw at her. But I've got nothing.

The perfect response will come to me in about five minutes.

"Anyway, do you know if Jonathan is coming tonight?" she asks, looking around. "I heard a rumor he might."

"I've been told that he's not coming," I replied, still trying to come up with something clever to say and failing.

Sarabeth shrugs. "Did Christopher tell you that?" She shakes her head. "I wouldn't believe a word that comes out of his mouth."

Again, I'm filled with anger, but nothing good to say. I decide I should just leave the conversation.

"If you'll excuse me, he promised me another dance." I turn and walk away from her, going directly to Christopher. I grab his arm and he shrugs to Donald as I pull him away.

"Thank you," he says once we're back out on the dance floor. "I wasn't sure how to get out of that."

"No problem," I tell him. "I wasn't particularly enjoying my conversation either."

He spins me around to the music. "Maybe this wasn't the best idea," he says. "Coming here, I mean."

"What? You don't think I can manage here?" I ask. I know Sarabeth is watching us and I am hyper aware of his hand on my hip. I remember the way his hand felt on my bare skin and I wish I didn't have a dress in the way.

"No. You are perfect," he tells me. "You could live this life."

I think of having to interact with Sarabeth all the time and shudder. "I'm not sure I want to."

He chuckles and spins me around, pulling me back close to him. "I don't blame you. Everyone here is a two-faced snake. They all want something."

"And you don't?"

"At least you know what I want," he replies with a wink.

Except I'm not sure I really do. I know he wants me away from his brother, but the way he holds me and the way he smiles at me both make me think that he wants me away from his brother for a more selfish reason than the merger. He says it's just business between us, but I'm beginning to wish it wasn't.

I could fall for Christopher if I let myself. If I thought he wanted me, that this could be more than just a pleasant way to spend our time together, I could easily fall in love with him. I already love his smile. When he laughs, my world is brighter.

It's everything I felt for Jonathan, only stronger. Only

real. I'm really with Christopher, but by a cruel twist of fate, I'm not sure if it's just the same silly crush as before.

"You want to get out of here?" Christopher asks.

"We just got here," I remind him.

"I already made the donation," he tells me. "We could go somewhere a little more private."

My breath catches in my chest and my stomach flutters. I didn't know how much I wanted to be alone with Christopher until just this moment.

"You sure?" I'm breathless and suddenly aching with desire for the man in my arms.

"You don't want to be here any more than I do," he says. "All of these people don't care if we're here. Let's go somewhere we can talk. Like we did on the island."

As if I could say no to that.

"Okay."

He grins, sending my heart into a fluttering mess. If he ever figures out what his smile can do to a woman, he'd make a million dollars. Then he'd be a billionaire with a little extra cash.

CHAPTER 20

"Here we are. It's not much, but it's home," Christopher says, holding open the door to his penthouse suite.

It's a stunning penthouse suite with iconic views of New York that is anything but "not much." The furniture is white and modern and there's art on the wall that I'm sure are original pieces and each one worth more than I paid for my college education. There's also a grand piano.

"Christopher, this is a museum-worthy piece of art that happens to be on top of a building," I tell him, standing in awe in front of the giant window that looks out over the twinkling city lights. From up here, it looks almost calm and peaceful.

"That's just because you haven't seen other people's," he tells me, going to the kitchen and opening the fridge. He pulls out a bottle of champagne and pops the cork.

I look around. I can't imagine how something could be more opulent than this. I suppose it could be bigger. More rooms or maybe painted with gold. The view alone has to be worth millions. It's something that the average person only sees once in a lifetime.

I can hear Christopher pouring champagne into cups. He growls as he knocks over one of the cups, spilling the champagne. I can see a wet mark spreading across his shirt. He sighs and gets another glass as I look around the house.

I can see little signs that this home is lived in. There's a book on the coffee table with a bookmark. And while there are no coffee cups in the sink or dirty laundry in the bedroom, there's still a feeling that someone lives here. There are photos on the wall of Christopher and his family in various parts of the world.

I look at the photos, smiling at the people I recognize. There are photos of Christopher and his mother, photos of Christopher and Jonathan, and one photo of them as a family with his father. Christopher looks happiest in that picture.

So much changed when Christopher's father died. Even though his mother was a partial owner, Christopher took over the company. With his father's death, responsibility and the weight of the company was suddenly solely on Christopher's shoulders. Jonathan wasn't old enough to quit school and go to work. That fell to the oldest son.

I wonder what kind of person Christopher would be if his father hadn't died. Would he be more carefree like Jonathan? Would he laugh more? Or would he still have dived into business with his entire being?

It didn't really matter. Christopher was the owner of a company set to be the world leader with this merger. So much of what Christopher had worked for all these years was riding on this merger with TimberTech.

I turn from the pictures. I was having such a nice time with Christopher that I forgot I was being managed. The only reason we went to the fundraiser was so that I wouldn't be near Jonathan. I remember Sarabeth telling me not to trust Christopher, and in the same breath asking if Jonathan was coming.

What if the reason we left the party wasn't because Christopher wanted to be alone with me? What if it was simply to keep me away from Jonathan?

"Here," Christopher says, handing me a glass of champagne. "To being managed."

I don't put my glass to his. Instead I stare down at the liquid for a moment before looking up at him.

"Christopher, what are we doing here?" I ask.

"Having a drink," he replies with a an easy shrug. He clinks his glass to mine and takes a sip.

"No, I mean us. Am I here because you're managing me, or..." My words catch in my throat a little. "Or is it something more?"

Christopher lowers his glass and his face grows serious. "I don't know."

I'm surprised at how much that hurts. It's not like I was expecting a declaration of love, but I was expecting something more.

"I like you, Nora," Christopher says softly. "I wouldn't have brought you to my home if I didn't."

"But?" I fight the urge to cross my arms.

"But, you're right. Business is a part of why you're here. If you weren't a distraction to the merger, to Jonathan..."

"Then I wouldn't be here." I turn from him and go to the window to look at the lights. They're beautiful out there, but they aren't helping me put my thoughts together. I play with my necklace, sliding it along the chain and feeling the metal catch and click under my fingers.

My heart aches. I know that I shouldn't expect anything from him. I know that the only reason I'm here is because I'm a threat to the merger. Yet, I still ache.

The ache tells me that I still want Christopher. I still want Christopher to want me. To crave the touch of my skin the way I crave his. Bitterness at the fact this isn't real creeps over me. The fact that I want it to be real, but that Christopher doesn't. That he see's this as business when it could be so much more.

I'll never tell him this. I can't.

This is business for him. It means nothing.

I feel his hands on my shoulders. His fingers are warm and I can't help but relax at his touch. He kisses the bare skin where my neck meets my shoulder. He's smooth shaven and his lips are soft. I close my eyes, my body remembering the way he felt on the island and already warming.

I want to feel this. I don't want to run from this, although I probably should. Despite my best efforts, I'm going to get my heart broken by Christopher. He doesn't feel the things I feel, yet I can't stop. I don't want to stop. Half of love is still better than no love.

As long as I keep it to myself, it won't hurt. My crush with Jonathan never hurt me. This will be no different. As long as Christopher thinks that I think it's business, he won't say anything to break my heart. All my emotions will stay safely in my head.

I turn to him. He's so damn handsome with those blue eyes and dark hair.

"I do like you, Nora. Very much." His eyes scan my face, absorbing every detail.

"You just don't like me with your brother." I don't know why I say it, but I do. I watch as hurt flickers across his face for just a moment.

"No, I don't," he agrees. His eyes go to mine. They are so blue the sky should be jealous. "But the reason I don't want you with him is more than just business."

My stomach twists, but I'm unsure if it's because his words make me happy or nervous. What if I'm wrong and there is something between us? What if he feels the same way about me and this isn't just two consenting adults having a good time, but something more?

"Is this how you manage all your business transactions?" I tease, trying not to think about what the implications of his last sentence could be.

He shakes his head slowly, a smile crossing his face for a moment. Then, he lowers his lips to mine.

"Just you. Although, I'd probably have better meeting attendance if I did," he whispers, right before he kisses me.

I forget about the world when he does that. His kiss transports me.

I put my hands inside his jacket and push it from his shoulders. He shrugs out of it and tosses it to the side. While still kissing him, I undo the buttons on his shirt.

I had planned to take my time. To ease into this, but now that we're kissing, I can't stop. My need is a runaway train. I can't stop. I can't get enough of him.

He shimmies out of the shirt and then breaks the kiss just long enough to pull the undershirt over his head. He tosses it to the side without a care.

I nibble my way down his jawline, feeling his shoulders flex beneath my fingers, a small moan of want escaping his perfect lips. I kiss his Adam's apple, down the the strong curve of his collarbone, down to one hard, erect nipple. He groans slightly, tangling his fingers in my hair as I take his nipple into my mouth.

Slowly, I work my way lower, kneeling in front of the bulge growing in his pants. With a wicked grin, I look up and unzip his dress pants. As the button comes undone and his pants fall away, his manhood stands ready for me. Inching the tux pants off his sculpted ass, followed quickly by his boxers and socks, I soon have him completely naked in front of me.

"Nora." His voice is gruff and full of tension. I look up to see him staring at me.

Now it's my turn to give him a cocky, sexy smile. I lick my lips and then take him into my mouth. I look at him through my eyelashes, watching him react with sheer pleasure. His groan heats my core to melting, but I don't stop. I rock gently back and forth, sucking and licking. He grows in my mouth, swelling with a need only I can meet.

His head falls back and his hands come to my hair. His fingers tangle in my hair as I work back and forth, savoring his taste and the obvious pleasure I'm giving him. He tenses for a moment, and then tugs gently on my hair.

"Not too fast," he tells me, coaxing me up to my feet. "Turn around."

I do as he asks and he kisses the back of my neck where it meets my shoulder. I shiver a little with anticipation, the sound of the zipper on my dress sliding down. I step out of the dress, leaving it a green puddle of satin and lace on the floor.

I turn and find him staring at me with eyes dark and

hungry, a need filling them that makes my heart beat harder. He reaches down and grabs the condom from his pocket and I grin. He came prepared this time.

I slide the bra straps from my shoulders, slowly removing the last few pieces of clothing. I tease him with my slowness, moving the bra away from my skin. I love the way his eyes dilate and focus on my chest. I'm not particularly well endowed, but his reaction makes me feel beautiful. I slide out of my lacy underwear and stand before him in nothing but my fancy high-heeled shoes.

He kisses me again, a no-holds-barred kiss that leaves me breathless. He pulls me to him, our naked bodies pressing together. Desire thrums through me like a strummed guitar string. His hands stroke my shoulders and then follow the curve of my breasts and hips.

His hands go to my waist and he picks me up, setting me on the nearby table. The wood is cool against my bare skin, but heat is coursing through me. I want him so badly I can think of nothing else.

He slides into me, my legs wrapping around his waist as he goes deep. I gasp at the wonderful sensation of him filling me to breaking. My nails dig into his back as he thrusts, his ass flexing and relaxing. I love the way his body feels as he pounds into me.

He growls, grabbing me by the hips and pulling me off the table. He spins me around so that my stomach is pressed against the table. He caresses the curve of my ass cheek before filling me once again. My hands splay against the smooth table top, my back arching to take more of him.

His speed increases, his hips bucking back and forth. His grip is hard on my hips, but only because he doesn't want me to stop. The primal sound of his breathing behind me is quite possibly the hottest thing I've ever heard.

It's going so fast. I don't want this to go this quickly, but at the same time my need for him is growing uncontrollable. I need him to crash into me.

"Don't stop," I plead, arching my back and begging for more.

He pushes harder, slamming into me hard enough to make the table shake. I love every moment of it and my eyes roll back into my head. We're coming together, fast and hard. There's no stopping us now.

He dives deep, his body filling mine and then exploding. I cry out with the sheer overwhelming pleasure of it all. I can't stop screaming his name as he fills me.

Slowly, he pulls back. He tugs on my hips, and helps me come back to standing. I'm glad he's holding me because I'm a little weak in the knees with pleasure.

"Thanks," I tell him, leaning into him.

He grins at me. "I'm not done yet."

My eyebrows raise and he chuckles. "Come with me."

He takes my hand and leads me to the bedroom. I don't know if my body can handle any more pleasure, but I'm sure willing to try and see if it can.

CHAPTER 21

The curtains are open on the windows. The filmy, translucent ones are pulled off to the side and the heavy-duty light blocking ones are tucked neatly at the ceiling. That means that the whole of New York City is spread out before us in a twinkling display as we lay in bed.

Combined with Christopher's naked body, it's the best post-sex view I've ever had.

I'm sweaty and satisfied. Parts of me ache from pleasure so great I didn't even know it was possible to feel that good. I thought the sex in the Caribbean was good, but this blows it out of the water.

I'm almost afraid to imagine how good the next session will be. Each time we have sex, it just gets better and better.

Christopher's phone rings in the other room. I realize it's still in his suit jacket that I threw on the floor. I'm fairly sure it's near the piano, but it could be on the couch. I wasn't paying much attention to the jacket once it was off him.

Christopher doesn't move.

"You going to get that?" I ask after the third ring. Given his nearly obsessive need to answer his phone, I'm sure he's had some sort of sex-induced stroke. I'm not looking forward to explaining that to his mother and the paramedics.

"Nope." Christopher wraps his arms around me, nuzzling his nose into my shoulder and giving me a small kiss. My heart thrills with the simple joy of it. I'm still buzzing on orgasm hormones, but it feels so good to be wrapped up in his arms. I'm safe here. I'm where I belong.

In the other room, the phone finally stops. And then it starts again. It goes through the cycle three times. I keep waiting for Christopher to get up, but he doesn't make a move. He just keeps holding me, ignoring his phone. I feel a warmth rise in me. Maybe there is something to our relationship. I try not to think about it because it will only make me hopeful and stupid.

The cell phone stops ringing and a new phone goes off. This one sounds like a real phone. It sounds like the one my grandmother keeps as a landline just in case she ever needs to dial 911.

"That one I am going to get," Christopher says. He frowns as he gets out of bed. I love watching him move. The muscles on his arms ripple and flex, and his torso is strong as he walks. It's like my own personal sexy show and he isn't even trying.

I hear his footsteps stop in the other room and the plastic sound of a phone being picked up. "This is Christopher."

He pauses for a moment, listening. I stretch out on the bed, a smile on my face. I can't believe how good I feel. I know that this is temporary, that this doesn't mean anything romantically to Christopher, but I'm not going to stop myself from enjoying it.

Just because he's managing me doesn't mean I can't be happy about it. As long as I keep my emotions to myself, I'll be fine. Christopher doesn't feel those emotions toward me, so it's better to pretend they don't exist.

If I don't acknowledge that I am falling for Christopher, then it isn't true. I'll be fine.

Christopher finishes the conversation and comes back to the bedroom. His eyes are dark and his face serious.

"What's the matter?" I ask, still lounging boneless in his bed.

"There's been an accident."

I sit up straight. All the happy, boneless feelings are gone. "What?"

"It's Jonathan." His voice trembles just a tiny bit on the end of his name. It's the sound of a worried older brother. It's the sound of fear.

My skin goes icy and I feel like I'm going to throw up.

"What happened?" I'm almost afraid to ask.

"He fell down some stairs," Christopher says. He walks over to his closet and opens the door. I can see rows of neatly pressed button-up shirts and suits. All the same, just different colors. All for work and nothing for pleasure. "We should go home."

I nod, scampering out of the bed and into the living room. I find my dress and underthings, hastily putting them on. I pull my hair back into a ponytail to keep it out of my face. I know I look a little bit like I'm doing the walk of shame, but since it's still date time, I don't have anything to be ashamed of.

I manage to mostly get myself back into the dress when Christopher comes out wearing fresh slacks and a new dress shirt. Since he spilled champagne on himself, I can't blame him for changing, but I am a little sad I don't get to look at him in his tuxedo anymore tonight. The man looks good in a tux.

We hurry down the elevator and Christopher has a car waiting to drive us back. Without wasting any time, we're whisked back to the mansion. I'm fairly sure that we're speeding, but Christopher can afford the tickets. We don't talk, both of us worried.

We spill out of the car and hurry to the main house. I'm right behind Christopher as he throws open the front door and stomps inside.

Jonathan is propped up on the couch, an ice pack resting on his head. My father is watching over him like a nervous hen. Dad is wearing his usual suit, but it looks like he threw it on. Half the buttons are undone and his hair isn't combed. He must have come over in a hurry.

Dad gives us both a once over and I see his mouth thin as he looks at Christopher. I'm still in my dress, but Christopher isn't in a tux. My dad isn't stupid. He'll figure it out, if he hasn't already. His eyes come back to me and he gives me the "what were you thinking!" look. Since he's working, it's rather subdued, but I'm sure I'll get an earful later. I'm just glad we're in front of the Family so he won't say anything right now.

"How is he, Doctor?" Christopher asks, coming to Jonathan's side. Dr. Wrigley is next to Jonathan, putting his stethoscope back into a leather bag. He's still wearing pajamas and looks like he was woken up to come in. Luckily, he only lives a few blocks away and is always on call for the Lewis family. Yet another perk of being rich.

"He's fine," Dr. Wrigley says. "He just tumbled down the stairs. Says he stumbled in the dark. I suspect alcohol may have been a factor."

"But he's okay?" Christopher asks. There's still a hint of worry in his voice that I find incredibly endearing. Despite it all, he does love his brother.

"I suspect a minor concussion. Keep him awake for the next few hours," Dr. Wrigley advises. He checks his bag and starts heading to the door. "After that, check on him every hour to make sure he wakes up."

"Of course, Doctor." Christopher nods.

"I've left all the instructions with Mr. Bailey," Dr. Wrigley says, giving a nod to my father. "I'll check in with Jonathan in the morning, but he should be completely fine."

"Thank you, Dr. Wrigley," Christopher says.

Dr. Wrigley nods and heads to the door. My father has a quick conversation, and Christopher goes to speak with Jonathan. I hang back, unsure of what my place should be in all of this. I don't really belong here, but I don't feel right just leaving either.

"Where's Mom?" Christopher asks Jonathan, coming to the side of the couch. He crouches down so he's at eye level with his brother.

"I thought she was with you at the party," Jonathan replies. He re-centers the ice pack on his head and frowns at Christopher. I try not to look guilty.

"We left early," Christopher says. He manages to

sound nonchalant and like we left the party and came straight here.

"Oh. I see."

For a moment, I think that maybe Jonathan believes him. That is until I see Jonathan focus in on Christopher's shirt. It's obviously not a tux, which means we made a stop.

"You should probably call her," Jonathan tells Christopher. "She'll hate that she's the last one to know."

"You're right." Christopher nods and stands up. He pulls out his phone and steps away from Jonathan to make the call to his mother.

"Am I allowed to have something to eat?" Jonathan asks, looking over at my dad. "The whole reason I came down the stairs in the first place was because I was hungry."

"Of course, sir." Dad snaps to attention. "What would you like?"

"A sandwich would be great," Jonathan replies. He gives my dad a smile. "You know what I like."

"Indeed I do." Dad pointedly looks over at me before heading into the kitchen. Once he's gone, it's just me and Jonathan in the living room. I can hear Christopher in the other room, still on the phone with his mother.

"So. You and Christopher, huh?" Jonathan looks up at me, one eye covered up with the corner of the ice pack.

I go and sit carefully on the edge of the couch near Jonathan's feet. "I don't really know how to answer that. It's not quite that simple."

Jonathan chuckles. "It's okay," he tells me. "I've stolen girls from him before. I definitely deserve it."

I smile, but there's not much joy in it. Christopher isn't

really with me. He's just keeping me busy so that Jonathan isn't with me. I don't feel right saying it out loud to Jonathan though.

"We never got our drink," Jonathan explains. "I probably shouldn't have any more champagne tonight, but for you, I'd risk it."

"I wouldn't want you to risk your health for me," I tell him. My heart is pounding in my chest. Even with a possible concussion, he's incredibly charming. I want to go for that drink, but I know I shouldn't. "Besides, I had drinks with Christopher tonight."

"Ah, that's how he stole my girl," Jonathan says, smiling at me.

My cheeks pink. Jonathan called me his girl. I'm suddenly incredibly flustered and seriously rethinking that drink.

"You know, we've done this before," Jonathan says.

"He's given you a concussion?" I ask, not quite following.

Jonathan laughs, the sound easy and light. "No, not the concussion. Just the girl stealing part."

"Oh?"

"Her name was Roxy." Jonathan frowns. "No, that's not it. Roxanne?" He squints slightly and then shakes his head. "No, it was Scarlet. Her name was Scarlet."

"Maybe Christopher stole all three from you," I reply.

"I stole her." Jonathan chuckles. He reaches over and touches my hand with his. "Christopher's not that good."

Just then, Christopher walks back in. Jonathan slowly pulls his hand away, but not before he's sure that his brother has seen him. Christopher's jaw tightens.

"Mother's on her way home. She's stuck in traffic." His

voice is low and calm, but his shoulders are tight. It doesn't help that his phone is buzzing like crazy in his hand.

"Go answer your phone, Christopher," Jonathan tells him. "It's probably important. It's always important with you."

Christopher's mouth tightens. He looks back and forth between Jonathan and me, and then turns to go back to the other room to answer his phone.

"You two look lovely, by the way," Jonathan says, watching his brother leave the room.

"Thank you," I say.

"Where did you and Christopher go tonight?" Jonathan asks, his voice friendly.

"A fundraiser. I forget what for, actually." I feel a little silly. It was my first major fundraiser and I didn't even know what I was there for.

"Was it the Blank Check Fundraiser?" he asks.

I nod, the name sounding familiar.

"I love that one," Jonathan tells me. "They always have the best band. Last year I helped out with the silent auction. It's a great organization."

I nod, thinking about how I danced with Christopher. It makes me smile. "The band was really good."

Jonathan nods and the ice pack slides off his head. It bounces off the couch and onto the floor. I can see a goose egg already forming on Jonathan's head and it makes me wince.

"I got it," I say, going to my knees on the floor and reaching for the ice pack. It's cold and slippery on my fingers as I put it back on Jonathan's forehead. I'm still on my knees in front of him. Our heads are nearly even since he's laying down.

He reaches out, catching my hand and holding it to his forehead. Our eyes meet.

If this were our love story, this would be the part where we kiss. This would be the part where the magic happens. I feel Jonathan move toward me. The kiss is coming. My heart pounds and my lips tremble...

CHAPTER 22

I pull away.

I don't know why I do it. I should want to kiss Jonathan. I've always wanted to kiss him. I've dreamed of kissing Jonathan.

Yet, I fumble back, pulling my hand out of his reach and rising to my feet. I don't kiss Jonathan Lewis despite my years of longing.

Teenage me would be furious with current me.

I cross the room and stand by the bookcase, my heart pounding in my chest. I feel like I might be sick. What am I doing?

Dad walks in with a sandwich and I'm even more glad I didn't kiss him. The last thing I need is for my dad to see me kissing Jonathan while Christopher isn't wearing the tux he left in. My hair is a mess and I'm sure I don't look like I came from a ball. I look like I came from bed.

Jonathan smiles at my dad as he hands him the sandwich. "You always make the best sandwiches," Jonathan tells him.

"Thank you, sir," Dad replies with a small smile. I see his shoulders straighten just a little bit with the compliment, though. The effect is spoiled by the yawn that overtakes my father. No matter how much butler poise and practice he has, a yawn is impossible to stop.

"You should go to bed, Dad," I tell him, putting my hand on his shoulder. I worry about him. Ever since that last cancer scare, I worry. I know that he needs his rest.

"The doctor said to keep Master Jonathan awake for the next two hours. Then to check on him hourly and make sure he's coherent when he wakes," Dad explains. He stifles another yawn. "I can't go to bed."

"I can do that. I can keep him awake," I tell him. "You go to bed, Dad."

Dad tries not to yawn again and fails miserably. I can see the tiredness in his eyes.

"Don't make me have Jonathan order you," I threaten. It's more of a joke, but I know that if Jonathan says it, Dad will go.

Dad knows this too. He glares at me.

"Go to bed," Jonathan says. "I'm sure Nora can handle me."

I can see the words "that's what I'm afraid of" nearly come out of Dad's mouth. He'd say them if we weren't in front of the Family. He glares at me, but since Jonathan said it, he has to do his duty and go to bed.

"If you need anything, I'm always available. I'll text you the instructions from the doctor." Dad turns and gives me one last hard look before heading out the front door and heading home for the night. I shake my head after him as he goes.

"Alone at last," Jonathan says, still looking cocky and sexy on the couch.

"Christopher is just out in the hallway," I remind him. I feel like it's important.

"He's on a work call," Jonathan replies. "He'll be busy for hours. We're basically alone."

I look out into the hallway. Christopher is pacing the marble floors as he holds the phone to his ear. He says something about the market reaction in Beijing, so I know Jonathan is right. If Christopher is doing business, he's off in his own world. He might as well be in Beijing himself.

"So, how are you going to distract me and keep me awake?" Jonathan asks. He flashes me a grin and waggles his eyebrows. "We could go play a little midnight tennis."

I roll my eyes. "I'm pretty sure that's against doctor's orders. No strenuous activity."

Jonathan grins wider. "For some reason, I think I could play nice and slow with you. I'm sure I can handle a little elevated heart rate."

I shake my head. "How about chess? I know my dad taught you how to play."

"He did." Jonathan looks surprised. "How'd you know that?"

"It was the summer you broke your collar bone," I tell him. "You were so unhappy you had to stay inside for a few days. I wanted to skip camp so I could come comfort you. Dad made me go to camp anyway."

I go to the cabinet on the far side of the room and pull out a beautiful wooden box. There's no dust to blow off the cover, so I take it to the coffee table in front of Jonathan and open it up.

"I remember that summer." Jonathan leans back against the pillow, his face thoughtful. "Your dad kept me sane. He'd come in and make a move every five minutes like clockwork. Even with all the extra time to think, I still couldn't beat him."

"Don't feel bad. I've had years to practice and I can't beat my dad." Piece by piece, I place the knights, queens, bishops and pawns on the board. I put the white pieces on Jonathan's side.

"You're giving me the advantage?" Jonathan asks, slowly sitting up so he can study the board better.

"You have a possible concussion," I remind him. "Seems fair."

He nods and reaches out to move a pawn. It's a fairly standard opening move for the game. "So, you and my brother."

I move my pawn in a mirror of his. "What about us?"

"Are you two a thing?" Jonathan moves a different pawn.

My hand hovers over the board, unsure of what piece I should move next. I should know, but I'm distracted by Jonathan's questions. "What do you mean?"

"Are you going to reply with a question to everything I ask?" Jonathan crosses his arms. "It's still your move, by the way."

I decide on a pawn. It seems like a safe move.

"You've been to his apartment." It's not a question from Jonathan. It's a statement. He moves another piece and watches my face.

"What makes you say that?" I ask, doing my best to sound innocent. I take my turn, moving a knight, hoping he's distracted and doesn't notice what I'm doing.

"See? Question again." Jonathan shakes his head. "And don't think I didn't notice you move that knight."

Darn.

"I know that you went to Christopher's place because he isn't wearing a tux, despite the fact that you two went to a black tie affair," Jonathan explains. He looks over the board as he speaks, evaluating the pieces like he just figured out Christopher and I. "The shirt he's wearing isn't one of his office shirts. Those are blue. That shirt is cream, which means it came from his apartment. You're still in your dress, so you didn't get the chance to change. Thus, *you* were at *his* apartment. It's elementary, my dear Watson."

He moves his piece with a little bit of flair.

"So I went to his apartment." I take my turn, setting up a trap for later. "So what?"

"So, that would make you the only woman other than his secretary and his cleaning lady to go inside," Jonathan explains. "He doesn't bring anyone there. All his dates, the few that are determined to try and tolerate him, end up at a hotel. He doesn't like letting anyone in."

"So you let everyone in to your apartment, but he lets no one in?"

"Ouch." Jonathan puts his hand to his heart in mock pain. "But true. I think we have issues. I think it's all related to the death of our father and the constant fear of being abandoned by the ones we love. You'd think we could afford a shrink or something." He grins and winks at me.

"It's your move," I tell him, pointing to the board.

"Right." He studies the board for a moment and moves a piece right where I want him to. "So, what are your intentions for my brother?" He looks up at me and chuckles. "I never thought I'd say that sentence."

"I'm just after his money," I say with a shrug.

Jonathan laughs. "There are easier ways to make money than dealing with Christopher." He focuses on me, his blue eyes intent. "But seriously. Do you like him?"

I fiddle with one of my chess pieces, not moving it on the board yet.

"He can't hear you out there," Jonathan tells me. "And I won't tell. Your secret is safe with me."

I sigh. "I do. I do like him," I tell him, still looking at the chess piece. I finally move it across the board. "I've really enjoyed spending time with him."

Jonathan nods. "And?"

I look up. "And what? He's only spending this time with me because I'm a threat to your engagement to Adeline, and thus his precious merger." I shake my head, surprised that not only am I saying this out loud, I'm saying it to Jonathan. "He's managing me. He's just making sure that I'm not going to be around you."

"Well, he's doing a great job." Jonathan moves his rook. "I mean, look how far apart we are right now."

I chuckle. My chess trap is almost ready. I move my piece. "His plan was working better the past couple of days."

Jonathan nods. "You two have been busy." He moves his pawn right where I want him to. "I heard you went to the Ocean Retreat. It's nice there. Lots of ways to keep busy."

"Keeping me busy is cheaper than paying me off," I tell him. I move my bishop.

"How much did he offer? Just curious."

"We never really got there. I just told him that I wouldn't accept money."

"Then he just didn't offer enough. Or... Or maybe his plan was to spend time with you all along."

I scoff. "Sure. Because I'm sure a billionaire has tons of free time." I take his rook.

"Hey!" He frowns at the board but then grins up at me. "It's okay, though. Check."

He moves his bishop and takes my queen.

My jaw drops open. I didn't see that coming at all. "You jerk."

"Just wait," he tells me with an evil grin.

I narrow my eyes and study the board. He has a couple of moves, but I don't see anything too dangerous to me. I see a way I can take out his other rook and put him in check. I do it.

"And you fell for it," he says triumphantly. He moves his queen. "Check mate."

"How did..." I stare at the board in shock. He has me. I never even saw it coming. "Where did you learn how to do that?"

"I dated a chess master for a week," Jonathan replies. "I picked up a few things."

I shake my head and look at the board. It's been a while since I've been trounced so quickly. My dad can't even beat me that fast any more. Jonathan is definitely smarter than he lets on to be.

"Play again?" I ask him.

He nods, glancing toward the open door. I can still hear Christopher on the phone in the hallway. Something about the Japanese markets this time.

I start to reset the board and realize that Jonathan still has my queen in his hand. "Will you hand me my queen?"

He looks down and nods. Somehow between me asking and him giving it to me, he drops it into the couch. I almost think it looks intentional, but I don't say anything. Either way, the couch cushions swallow it up.

"Sorry," Jonathan says, peering down at the couch. "It appears the couch ate it. Help me find it?"

I go around the coffee table and we both get on our knees in front of the couch. I lift up one of the couch cushions and start looking for my missing piece.

"That's it, keep going," Jonathan moans. I look over at him, totally confused.

"What are you doing?" I ask. His concussion must be worse than I thought.

"This," he tells me, motioning his head toward the hallway.

Two seconds later, Christopher is standing there, hand over the mouth of his phone and looking a combination of concerned and angry.

"Hey bro." Jonathan says, looking completely pleased with himself.

CHAPTER 23

"What's going on in here?" Christopher asks, his eyes going back and forth between Jonathan and me.

"Just looking for a missing chess piece," Jonathan tells him with a smug smile.

"That's not what it sounded like," Christopher tells him, his voice low and dangerous.

I see the piece near the back of the couch, grab it, and hold it up triumphantly. "Found it."

"What are you two doing?" Christopher asks. His hand is still over the mouthpiece of his phone and his eyes are flashing.

"Playing strip chess, obviously," Jonathan replies. I could smack him.

Christopher's eyes go wide and he looks over at me.

"Wait. Just regular chess," Jonathan amends. "She still has her dress on despite the fact that I'm winning."

I really could smack him this time, but instead I just roll my eyes.

"I'm seriously doubting the doctor's concerns about a concussion," I tell him. "You're doing just fine."

I roll up onto my toes and then up to standing. I walk deliberately back to the opposite side of the coffee table and place my queen before taking my seat.

Christopher still hasn't moved. He's still standing in the doorway, framed by yellow light from the hall. His eyes bounce between Jonathan and me and frustration vibrates off of him.

"You can go back to work. I promise that all we're doing is playing chess," Jonathan tells him. "And I won't even press for strip chess on the next game."

Christopher glares at Jonathan. The two of them have a conversation with their eyes. It reminds me of the meeting in the bar. Jonathan smirks and Christopher looks angry. Finally, Christopher's jaw clenches twice. "Fine," he growls, and then spins on his heel and out of the room.

I can hear him in the hallway again. He sounds angry on the phone this time.

"What was that all about?" I ask Jonathan, glaring at him. I don't like that he purposefully tried to anger his brother. "Did you really have to antagonize him like that?"

"I was just seeing how closely he was listening to us in here," Jonathan replies with an innocent shrug. "The rest was just our regular brother stuff."

"He really wants this merger," I tell him. "If you do anything with me and alienate Adeline, it's off. That's why he was listening. He doesn't want me screwing things up."

"Screwing definitely has something to do with it. But not just the merger," Jonathan agrees. Before I can reply he tells me, "You can be white this time. You need every advantage you can get."

I spin the board so I have the white pieces this time. I make the first move. My mind isn't fully on the game though. I'm not entirely sure what Jonathan means by "not just the merger."

I know that Christopher came into the room because Jonathan made it sound like we were getting busy. He would have come rushing in with any girl in the room, not just me. He wanted this merger and wasn't going to let anyone stand in his way.

He didn't come in the room because it was me. He came in the room because of Jonathan.

"You asked me about Christopher. I should ask you about Adeline," I say, waiting for Jonathan to move his piece.

"What about Adeline?" he asks. He moves a pawn to match mine.

"Do you love her?" I move my pawn.

He thinks for a moment, then matches my move. "You know, it terrifies me, but I do."

I raise my eyebrows at him. "And that's why you wanted to have dinner with me at the conference?"

"I've never felt this way about anyone. I'm not used to it. There's never been any desire to have something permanent before," he tells me, not really answering my question. "I don't know what to do with that."

"I'm sure the merger helps," I say, moving a piece on the board.

"It's not just the merger. It's her." Jonathan smiles, his eyes going soft and distant. "Even without the merger, I think I would still want it to be permanent. Or, at least I think I do. It's a very new sensation for me."

"Your move," I tell him.

"It's a good thing I have Christopher, or I'd screw it up." He moves one of his knights. "I'd throw something amazing away because I'm scared that someone could love me like that. I think I don't know how to be happy sometimes."

"And thus why you had dinner with me," I say with a a sigh.

He nods. "Sorry. You'd be great sabotage. I like you a lot." He sighs and shrugs. "I just like her better. Which is terrifying. I've never felt this way about anyone before."

"I think it's sweet," I tell him, taking my turn.

"Just what I want to hear. Men love being told they're *sweet*." Jonathan curls up his lip in disdain. He sets down his chess piece a little harder than necessary.

I chuckle. "But it is," I tell him. "I'm a little jealous, actually."

"Jealous?" Jonathan looks surprised. "Of me being terrified? Love is not as easy as it looks."

"Just that you've found it, even if it's not with me," I reply. I give him a rueful grin. I might as well admit all my secrets to him at this point. "I've kind of had a crush on you since forever."

"Really?" Jonathan grins. "There's a boost to my ego."

"As if you needed one," I say with a roll of my eyes. "You didn't know?"

He shakes his head. "If I did, I would have taken advantage of it a long time ago."

"That's probably why my father kept sending me off to camp. And all the after school activities I could manage," I say with a laugh.

"It's probably why I was banned from the kitchen," Jonathan says.

"That's where I did my homework," I tell him.

We look at each other and smile.

"Maybe in another life we'll get together," Jonathan says. "But in this one, I have Adeline. And you have Christopher."

"I have Christopher?" I scoff and shake my head. I move my knight. "As soon as his precious merger is safe, he'll drop me like a hot stone. I'm not under any illusions."

"Nora, he brought you to his house," Jonathan says like it means something. "He likes you."

I shake my head. "You say that, but..." I sigh. "It's your move."

Jonathan moves his piece without looking at the board. "He likes you. A lot."

I look up at Jonathan. He's earnest and sure of his appraisal of his brother. He doesn't look like he's playing a trick on me, and I can't think of a reason why he would.

"You think so? You think it's not just an act to keep me away from you?" I ask, crossing my arms. "Why?"

"I've never seen my brother act like this," he says, motioning to the hallway. "And not to mention, I've never seen him this happy. He's been... smiley. My brother does not do smiley. Angry, nonchalant, bored, indifferent, intense- but never smiley."

"So?" I shrug. "We went to a beach. Maybe he's just happy he got some."

"He's gotten plenty and never acts like that," Jonathan assures me. "If he did, I'd be making sure he got a lot more sexy times. If it was that easy to make him smiley, I'd go on dates for him."

I move my chess piece and try not to think about Christopher having sexy times with other people. It stirs something dark and uncomfortable that looks a lot like bitter jealousy in my stomach.

"I think the feelings you two have are real." Jonathan shrugs. He takes his turn. "Christopher keeps his emotions closed off, but I've never seen him let anyone get as close to him are you have. I've never seen him rush into a room that angry before."

"You've never seen your brother trying to keep a five billion dollar merger from falling apart either," I reply. I move my knight and take his pawn.

"It's real," Jonathan assures me. "I know my brother. He's in love with you."

While Jonathan evaluates the board, I try to evaluate my emotions. My heart is threatening to explode in my chest. What if this time, these things I feel with Christopher is real? What if Christopher actually has feelings for me?

I haven't let myself think of the possibility of us as a couple. I know I'm falling for him, but I don't want to be played a fool. If I keep telling myself that it's not real, then I won't get hurt when it isn't. If I don't admit I'm in love, I'm hoping it will hurt less when it ends. I've been dreading the day the merger happens because it means that Christopher won't stay with me.

But if Christopher does have feelings for me, then that changes things. If Christopher loves me, then I won't get hurt if I tell him how I feel. The merger won't be the end of us.

We could have a future together.

I love the idea of a future with Christopher. I can see us having adventures and curling up on the couch during a snowstorm. I can see us laughing and playing. There is a beautiful future for us, if the things I feel aren't all just on my side.

I look up at Jonathan and he smiles at me. He gives me a confident nod. Hope fills me from the toes up. I can't stop smiling. I look over at the doorway, expecting to see Christopher there, but it's empty. I don't hear his voice on the phone, but that doesn't mean anything. I grin over at Jonathan.

"What should I do?" I ask him.

Jonathan moves his rook and takes out my queen. "Don't play strip chess with me."

CHAPTER 24

"Jonathan! Jonathan, are you okay!?"

Deborah rushes into the room, her silk scarf trailing after her like a streamer. She rushes past me, nearly knocking me over even though I'm already sitting down on the floor. She gets to her son, and puts her hands on his cheeks, inspecting him for damage.

"I'm fine, Mom," he tells her with a chuckle. "You nearly took out Nora."

"Nora?" Deborah looks back at me surprised. "I'm sorry, dear. I didn't see you."

"It's fine," I tell her.

I am the butler's daughter after all. I'm not meant to be seen.

"I am going to stay up all night with you," Deborah tells Jonathan. "Dr. Wrigley told me exactly what I need to do."

"I guess you're off the hook, Nora," Jonathan says to me.

"You just don't want to lose another game of chess to me," I tease him. I won the game just before Deborah came home, but only barely. Jonathan has a keen mind and is good at strategy. He'd be so good at business if he decided to help his older brother out.

Jonathan laughs. "We'll have to play again sometime," he tells me.

"So I can beat you again?" I grin at him.

He laughs. "I had to let you win. It's all part of my bigger strategy. Boost your confidence so I can destroy you easier next time."

He winks at me and I grin back at him. I think I'll always be a little bit in love with him, but I know that it won't ever be real. He's just too charming not to love at least a little bit.

"Let's get you to bed," Deborah says, glancing over at me like I might steal her son away at any moment. "You should rest. Adeline will be so worried about you."

With his mother holding his arm like he might fall down at any moment, he goes upstairs and to his room. He rolls his eyes as he passes me, but he lets his mother help. It's a small thing, but it will make Deborah happy.

I watch the two of them go up the stairs, then I clean up the board game and put it away. Once everything is how my father would want the room to look, I go and find Christopher.

Christopher is sitting at the head of the dining room table. The Lewis family hosts massive dinner parties in this room. The large room has gilded windows, gilded ornate chairs, and golden curtains. There's heavy golden candlesticks on the golden table cloth. Even as a child I thought it looked like King Midas had gone through the room.

Christopher looks like a weary king on a throne. The carved golden curls on the chair sit over his head like a crown, but there's a weight on his shoulders that makes me want to hug him. He looks tired and worn. I wonder just what bad news about business he learned tonight.

"How's business?" I ask, coming around the table.

"Fine." He pockets his phone and stands.

"You okay?" I ask, reaching out to touch his shoulder.

He pivots away from me, taking a step in the opposite direction so I don't touch him. "Fine."

I frown slightly, trying not to feel hurt. It must have been worse news than I thought.

"How's Jonathan?" Christopher asks.

"He's good," I reply. "He nearly beat me in chess twice. I don't think he has much of a concussion. I had to use every trick I know to win the second time."

"He looked happy." Christopher looks at me, his voice strained.

"Well, that's because he was winning," I inform him. "He didn't look so happy when I won."

Christopher shakes his head, a sad smile on his face. "No, it was more than that. You both looked happy."

"Are you okay?" I ask taking a step toward him. "You look like someone kicked your dog."

He rubs his temples and closes his eyes for a moment. "Just business," he tells me. "The merger. There's a snag I was trying to avoid."

"Well, you will be glad to know that Jonathan assures me he's going to marry Adeline. It's actually pretty sweet the way he talks about her." I smile at Christopher, thinking that this will be welcome news.

"Of course it's sweet. That's Jonathan's basic tactic," Christopher sighs and shakes his head. "It's Scarlet all over again."

"What do you mean?" I ask. I remember Jonathan saying something about Scarlet and stealing her away from Christopher, but that was a long time ago.

"I should get you home," Christopher says, changing the subject.

"Oh. Okay." I nod, but I didn't really want the night to be over just yet. I was hoping that Christopher and I could go somewhere and make-out. I feel like a teenager in love for the first time and I want to enjoy this sensation with him. Jonathan thinks that Christopher actually likes me, and I am willing to take the risk on Christopher if that's true.

However, Christopher looks exhausted. As much as I want to spend time with him, I also want him to be happy, healthy, and not stressed. Some sleep would do him good.

"I should let you rest," I tell him. "You look beat. I can get home myself."

"I'll walk you," he says firmly. "You know, for safety."

"Because it's such a bad neighborhood," I tease him. "You never know about those pesky millionaire neighbors trying to sneak into your pool area and steal your prize winning gardenias."

He cracks a smile, but it quickly fades from his eyes. He guides me to the front door and we step outside.

The night air is humid and warm. It feels good after the air conditioned cold of the house. I take a deep breath in, smelling jasmine and the lingering scent of cut grass. The crickets and frogs are so loud I can barely hear the sound of our footsteps on the crushed gravel path. The moon is out, lighting our way, but even if it wasn't there's discrete solar lights lining the pathways.

No pesky millionaires jump out at us on the short walk to my father's home above the garage. We pause together at the bottom of the stairs.

"Thank you for a lovely night, Christopher," I say.

I go to my tiptoes to kiss him, giving him a goodnight kiss. He wraps his arms around me, holding me so tightly I'm afraid I might burst. I kiss him, loving the way he tastes. I sigh when he pulls away.

"Goodnight, Nora." He lets me go, his hand staying on my shoulder for an extra second.

I turn and take two steps up the stairs.

"Nora?" he calls. I turn, ready to run down the stairs if he wants. "Will you come to the office tomorrow afternoon?"

"Um, sure." That wasn't the question I was expecting. "What do you need?"

"Some more paperwork on the hotel came in," he tells me. "I was hoping you could look at it and sign a couple of things. Just to make everything formal."

"Sure." I smile warmly at him, already looking forward to seeing him again. "What time do you want me to come?"

"You're welcome anytime."

My heart trembles at that sentence. Maybe Jonathan is right. Maybe Christopher does like me more than just a friend.

"Does two work?" I ask.

He nods. "Two is perfect."

"Do you want me to bring lunch?"

He shakes his head. "No. There's food at the office. My secretary gets sandwiches from the deli downstairs. I'll have her get you one too."

"Thank you." I smile and walk back down the two stairs. "I like turkey."

And then I kiss him on the cheek. There's a hint of stubble there now and I love it. It's masculine and relaxed. It's like my secret version of Christopher. He closes his eyes.

"Thanks for letting me sit with Jonathan this evening," I tell him. "It was good for both of us."

"Anything for Jonathan," Christopher says softly. He slowly opens his eyes and looks at me. He reaches out and gently touches my cheek, his fingertips so light I can barely feel them. He looks like he has something he wants to say, but then he shakes his head. "Goodnight, Nora."

"Goodnight, Christopher." I wait for a moment to see what might happen, but he steps away from me. I nod and head up the stairs. The door creaks slightly as I enter and I look back at Christopher. He gives me a small wave from the bottom of the stairs.

I close the door and go inside. I can still see him through the window. He stands at the bottom of the stairs for a long moment. I see him take a deep breath and look up at the house. He doesn't see me in the window, but he looks sad. He sighs and heads back to the main house.

His steps are slow and methodical. He stops once and looks back, but then just keeps walking.

"You seem happy this morning," Dad says as I slide into the small kitchen and make myself a cup of coffee.

I'm humming and I did my hair and makeup today. I even have on a cute dress, so I have to agree with him. I am happy.

"I had a good night," I tell my dad.

"With Jonathan?" Dad asks, doing his best to keep judgment out of his voice.

"No, with Christopher."

Dad sets down the morning paper. "Christopher?"

I nod. "I'm going to go meet him at the office after lunch." I wince at the hot coffee. "I need to run some errands first."

"Why does Christopher have an interest in you?" Dad asks, his eyes narrowed.

"Because I'm smart, pretty, and very amusing," I tell him.

"While all true, those aren't usually Christopher's reasons

for having an interest in people," Dad replies. "He's all business. He was that way as a child and it's only gotten worse since his dad died. He never does anything without a reason."

I think of how those words are the same ones playing in my head, but then I remember Jonathan telling me that Christopher obviously has feelings for me. That Christopher loves me. I want Jonathan to be right. I *feel* like Jonathan is right.

"I think you might be too hard on him, Dad." I sip at my coffee and lean against the counter.

"I'm a father. I'm supposed to be hard on anyone interested in my daughter." He frowns. "But you're right. Christopher isn't all bad. He gives a good Christmas bonus."

I give Dad a withering gaze.

"I know he donates to charity, too," Dad adds.

"Wow." I roll my eyes. "Such high praise."

Dad ignores my sarcasm. "You need to be careful with the Lewis men," he says, looking at me with stern eyes. "Neither of them know how to love. Jonathan flits between serious relationships, but never stays in one long enough to find happiness, but he also never gets hurt. Christopher is the other side of that coin. He avoids all relationships so he never can find happiness, but again, never gets hurt."

"So you're saying they'll never know love?" I ask him.

"No, they could. Love has the power to overcome anything," he tells me. "But be careful. They only write down the love stories with happy endings. There are many more that end in heartbreak that never make it to the page. Not every love story ends with a happy ending."

"Thanks for the warning, Dad."

"That's my job. I am king of warnings." He smiles at me. "And I'll sit out on the porch with a shotgun if necessary, because I am your father and that is a love story that will be written down."

For all our arguments and faults, my father loves me completely.

I set down my coffee on the table and give my dad a kiss on the cheek.

"I love you, Dad," I tell him. He smiles up at me. "I'll see you later."

"Mmm hmm," he grumbles, giving me a grumpy smile before picking up the paper again. I grab my bag and head outside.

I take the train into the city. It's definitely a different experience than riding in a limo. The sights are different, the company is different, and the smells are most certainly different. The summer sun reflects off skyscraper windows as I enter the concrete jungle.

Everywhere I look, people are on their phones. I'm reminded that I haven't talked to Julie for a few days and I promised to call. There's so much to update her on.

"This is Julie," she says on the third ring. Hearing her voice makes me smile.

"Guess who?" I say, keeping the phone pressed to my ear as I look into windows as I walk past stores.

"Nora! What is going on? You have to tell me everything!" I can practically hear her grin through the phone. "Tell me what's happening with Jonathan!"

"Well, he ran into me at the conference. We had dinner," I reply.

"Shut up! And you didn't call me right away?"

"Sorry," I say, feeling a little guilty. "It's been a busy week. I think I'm falling in love."

I proceed to tell her the entire story of the week from the dinner to the Caribbean hotel to last night playing chess. I tell her how I don't feel the same intensity toward Jonathan. I tell her that I now feel it for Christopher.

"Well. That's not how I saw this phone call going at all," Julie tells me once I've finished. "Christopher? Really?"

"I know, right?" I shake my head. "But he's actually amazing. He's just got a shell. He's got layers."

"Like an ogre?"

I roll my eyes. "I know I didn't paint him in the best light when I first told you about him." I stop and look into a jewelry store. The front window is full of sparkling engagement rings. For the first time, it's not Jonathan that I want one from. "He's actually smart and funny. We get along really well."

"Do you love him?" Julie asks.

I look at the rings and I can see Christopher giving me one. I can see a beautiful future for the two of us. I don't need a ring right now, but maybe in a few years?

"I do," I tell her. "I actually really do."

"I'm not sure he deserves you," Julie replies. "But if he makes you as happy as you sound, then I say go for it."

"But what if he doesn't feel the same about me?" I ask her, turning away from the rings. I continue walking. "I know Jonathan thinks there's feelings there, but..."

"Has Jonathan ever been wrong?" Julie asks.

I think back. Jonathan is usually the people person. I've actually never seen him read a person wrong. He always knows what to say and how to say it. He's got people skills. I remember he once got his aunt a puppy one year for her birthday. Everyone said it was a terrible idea, but he did it anyway. He was right. The aunt loved the dog. It was her favorite gift and he became her favorite nephew from that moment on.

"He's always been right about people," I tell Julie.

"Then he's probably right about his brother," she informs me. "Besides, I can hear it in your voice how happy you are. You're a pretty good judge of character yourself. What would you tell yourself?"

I try to think about my situation from an outside perspective. I look at what Christopher has said and done. The time he's spent with me. The way his attention focuses on me. The small things, like how he sits close to me and the big things, like not answering his phone the other night.

"So what do I do next?" I ask Julie.

"Tell him how you feel," Julie advises. "That's the next logical step. You don't have to drop the L-word on him just yet, but you can tell him that you really like him. That you want to take this relationship further."

My stomach twists with nerves at the idea. The idea that I might put myself out there and reveal that I didn't keep this a consenting adults thing like he wanted makes me nervous. While I don't think he'll reject me, the idea that it could happen terrifies me.

I can slightly understand why Jonathan kept asking me to the pool house. It would be easier to run from this. To find someone who didn't scare me with the depth of my feelings. The fear of rejection from someone I truly love is more terrifying than jumping out of an airplane.

At least I might survive jumping out of an airplane. If

I'm rejected, I don't know if my heart will ever be the same.

"You think I should?" I chew on my lower lip. "Maybe I should keep it to myself for a little while still. He's got a lot on his plate. I don't want to complicate things."

"You do what feels right," Julie says. "You'll know the right time to tell him. It'll feel natural."

"Okay." I nod, even though she can't see me.

"Hey, I have to go back to work," Julie says. I can hear conversations in the background. "Call and tell me everything when you get a chance!"

"I will," I promise.

"And no waiting a week for the good stuff," she tells me sternly.

"Yes, ma'am." I grin, and promise myself that I won't wait again. "Have a good day!"

Julie says goodbye and the phone line goes quiet. I carefully put it back in my pocket. I still have a little time before I'm supposed to meet with Christopher.

There is a couple walking in front of me on the street. They're hand in hand and smiling. There's not a care in the world for the two of them.

I know that feeling, and I find that I'm not envious. I'm happy for them. I have that feeling. I have no reason to be jealous or wish for it myself. I have it. I love Christopher.

I stop dead in the center of the street with the realization that this is real. My feelings are real. That every bone in my body says that Christopher returns them and that we have the same something special as the couple walking ahead of me.

A taxi honks angrily at me and I hurry out of the street.

I grin as I walk. Christopher brought me to his house.

He pays attention to me. He takes time out of his busy day to see me. The man is planning a multi-billion dollar merger, yet he has time to see me. He has time to take me out on a date. His time is worth millions, yet he spent it with me.

Even a money-hungry billionaire wouldn't waste time on that if he didn't want to. He could have sent an underling or his mother to take me to the fundraiser and away from Jonathan. The fact that he did it himself meant that he feels something for me too.

Warmth bubbles up from the tips of my toes all the way to the top of my head. Sunshine doesn't feel this good. The only thing that feels this good is Christopher's arms around me and his lips on mine.

I want to dance down the streets of the city and shout it from the top of the Empire State Building.

I love Christopher and he loves me.

CHAPTER 26

I finish running my errands and window shop a little more as I work my way through the city until it's suddenly two o'clock and time for me to meet with Christopher. I can't wait to see him. My heart is bursting with love.

I ride up in a silver elevator to Christopher's floor. I'm always amazed at how beautiful a concrete and glass building can be. It's not as pretty as a mountain or the ocean, but it's still magnificent and grand in its own way.

I'm a little late, but not so much that I feel the need to call ahead. Besides, we said two-ish, so I'm in the clear. I check in with his secretary and she buzzes me into his office.

Christopher's office is immense. It's bigger than any apartment I've ever lived in. There's a full marble bathroom complete with shower and fancy toilet. My father tells me that there's a pull-out bed in the sofa on the far side of the room. There's also a closet full of clothes. Theoretically, Christopher could live in this office and never have to leave as long as his secretary brings him food once in a while.

Christopher sits behind a giant mahogany desk with the big windows overlooking the city behind him. He looks up when I enter and smiles. The smile hits me so hard I stagger with its beauty. When the man wants to, he really can make a woman go weak in the knees with just a look.

"Hi." He stands up to greet me and I notice he's still wearing the same shirt as last night. He hasn't changed.

"Hi," I reply. "Did you sleep at all? Or have you been working all night?"

"I guess I didn't change." He looks down at his shirt and shrugs. "I couldn't sleep, so I thought I'd get some work done. With the merger coming up, there's always a million things to do."

"I guess. Don't work too hard, though. That's how you get sick," I tell him.

"I'll worry about that after the merger," he replies. "Have you seen Jonathan today?"

I shake my head. "When I left the house, everyone was still sleeping. I've been in the city all morning."

He nods. "That's good."

I walk across the big office, planning on kissing him. I'm still giddy with the idea that Christopher does feel something for me. I can't seem to get Jonathan's words out of my head. Christopher is in love with me.

Christopher goes back behind his desk before I can reach him. "I have the papers for you."

He rifles through a stack of things on his desk, finally pulling out thick stack of papers. He hands them to me over the desk.

On the top of the papers is an envelope. It's paper-clipped to the first page of the file beneath it, but my name is neatly printed on the envelope. I look up at Christopher with a questioning frown.

"Open it," he tells me.

I set the stack of papers down on a bare corner of Christopher's desk and peel open the envelope. It's an itinerary for a private flight to the Caribbean, specifically the island we went to earlier this week. The same room is booked, as well as scuba diving and a dolphin encounter. The plane leaves tomorrow.

"What is this?" I ask, not understanding what I have in my hands. I don't need to be managed anymore. I'm no longer a threat to Jonathan.

"A vacation," he tells me. "Sort of. There's more than just the itinerary there. I bought it. The hotel."

I look down at the paperwork that had been underneath the envelope and see that indeed he has. "Congratulations!"

"You convinced me," he says with a small shrug and a smile.

I look down and realize that my name is now in one of the owner positions. I blink, thinking that I have to be reading it wrong. Why would my name be next to Christopher's?

"Why is my name as a partial owner?" I ask. "That can't be right."

"It is," he tells me. "Just ten percent. If the hotel is successful, you'll get more as time goes on. It's all in that contract."

The air leaves my lungs. I stagger back, luckily finding the chair just as my knees go out. I stare down at my name as an owner of a hotel in the Caribbean. It's the future I've dreamed of for years now. I never thought it would ever actually happen, and if it did, I expected it to be years in the future. But there is my name as an owner of a hotel.

"Christopher, I don't know what to say," I gasp. My hands shake as I look at the papers.

"Then don't say anything. I just want you to be happy."

I stand up and kiss him. His hair slides through my fingers and I love the way his arms wrap around my waist. I moan a little, his kiss better than chocolate, and I love the way his arms tighten. The man knows how to kiss.

When we break from the kiss, I look up at him with happy tears in my eyes. "You just gave me my dreams. How could I not be happy?"

"You leave tomorrow." Christopher smiles, but it's not one of his real ones. It's not a make my-knees-wobble smile. It's a business smile.

"You okay?" I ask him.

"Yeah. I'm fine." He breaks the embrace and goes back around to the far side of his desk. "Just stressed."

"Then it's a good thing you have a vacation coming up." I grin at him.

"Vacation?" he asks.

"Well, you need to come with me, of course. You're an owner. I'll want to go over some staffing decisions with you, but we can do that after the dolphin encounter. And before we get too busy in bed."

He smiles wistfully, as if imagining us in bed together again. "Nora, I'd love to come with you. I really would. But the merger..."

My heart sinks. "You're not coming?"

He shakes his head. "I'll join you as soon as the merger is complete, but there's just no way I can break away."

"But I can call you, right?" I say with a little pout. I don't really want to go to the island and do all the fun things alone.

He patted his phone with a smile. "I always have my phone on me."

I think about it for a minute. This is the life that I'll have to get used to. Still, he is offering me my dream job and telling me he's going to be there with me soon.

I smile. "We should celebrate."

"Celebrate?" he says, sounding unsure.

"I think you promised me a sandwich," I remind him. "I think a celebration sandwich is in order."

"I did, didn't I?' He chuckles and shakes his head. "I should follow through on at least some of my promises."

Christopher stands up and goes to a small fridge on the side of his office. I follow him with my eyes, not quite sure what he means by "some of his promises." It seems a strange thing to say, but then I'm still so flustered and excited about my new hotel that I can't think straight.

He looks inside his fridge, and for a moment seems confused. He pulls out only one sandwich. "I think my secretary must have brought your sandwich to her own fridge." Just then, his phone rings. He looks at me with a pained expression.

"Go on, answer it," I say. "I can find my celebration sandwich."

He smiles, then answers the phone. I leave his office and ask the secretary if she got an extra sandwich. She smiles and hands me it out of her fridge.

I quietly open the door to Christopher's office, careful not to make too much sound while he's on the phone. He's standing at the window, one hand in his pocket, looking out at the city while talking on the phone.

"Uh huh. Uh huh. Yeah. No, she won't be a problem anymore. Yeah, she took it. It was easier than I ever thought it would be. Cheaper too. Much cheaper than the six million you suggested I offer."

Is he talking about me? I think to myself.

"She'll be out of here tomorrow morning on my jet. And she'll be busy enough that she won't have a chance to come back before the wedding. The merger is all set. The problem has been taken care of."

I think of the flight itinerary that had been in that envelope. He's definitely talking about me. I was the problem.

I close the door loudly. He turns back to me and smiles, unaware that I've heard anything. "Hey listen, I'll call you back with those projections later. I'm going to have a bite of lunch now." He hangs up the phone and puts it in his pocket.

I try to smile, but I can't.

I follow him to a small table on the side of his office with two chairs. I unwrap my sandwich and find fluffy white bread, thick tomatoes, pickles, cheese, and piled with turkey. It's huge, and very New York deli.

It looks delicious. I know I won't be able to eat a bite.

"So, when do you think you will be able to come out to the island?" I ask.

He shrugs, as if he's not lying to my face. "It's hard to say. There's still some regulatory hoops we need to jump through. Logistical problems. Eliminating some redundant positions once it's official."

I smile but it's not real. "You didn't answer my question."

"It's really impossible to say, Nora. If I had to put a guess on it, I'd say the earliest I could break away for a day would be four weeks."

"I see," I say. "And could I come visit you before then?"

He freezes, as if he didn't expect the question. "I'd love

that, Nora, but aren't you going to be pretty busy? It's not everyday you get put in charge of a Caribbean hotel."

"Surely I'm not going to be as busy as you," I say. I take a bite of the sandwich. It would be a shame for the entire thing to go to waste. "After all, you were able to take a couple days off even with this merger going on."

He stayed frozen. "I think it would be best if you concentrated on the hotel. I'm still 90% owner of it and I'd love for it to turn a bigger profit."

"Bigger profit? So it's all just business for you?" I ask, my voice rising in both pitch and volume.

He sighs. "How much did you hear?"

"Enough," I say. "How long were you going to string me along?"

He shakes his head, and for a moment I think he's going to deny the whole thing. "Nora, I can't... I didn't..."

"You never planned on coming to the island again, did you?" Dread starts to trickle into the pit of my stomach.

"Stop, Nora." Christopher holds up his hand, his face dark.

I look up at him, my heart trembling. This isn't how I saw this going. Was Jonathan wrong about his brother's feelings toward me? "What?"

"I can't do this," he says softly, turning away from me. He shakes his head and takes a deep breath. When he turns around, his smile and bright eyes are gone. All that's left is the businessman. He straightens up, his hands behind his back in a formal pose.

"I'm not coming with you to the island," he admits, his voice flat.

"But why?" I ask.

"It was always about the merger and keeping you away

from Jonathan." His body stays rigid and unyielding. "You will go to the resort. You will stay there until the merger is over."

"And then you'll join me, right?" I ask with a small voice. "Jonathan said you don't bring anyone to your apartment, but I was there. That has to mean something. I must mean something?"

There's still hope that my heart isn't going to be crushed. I feel it cracking, but I'm hoping that this is just a misunderstanding. That he's just going to be late or that he needs to do a few things first.

I don't want to be wrong about him. I've let myself start to feel things for him and now I can't stop. I took the risk. Now I'm afraid it was the wrong thing to do. That it was a stupid thing to do.

"No." His eyes are cold. "You asked if I was managing you. I am. I have been all week. It's all I've been doing. I've been keeping you away from my brother by any means necessary."

"What do you mean?" I slide off his desk. My legs are shaky, but I'd rather be on my own two feet than perched on the desk. I want to stand on my own. Plus, it would help if I need to run.

Christopher squares his shoulders. He has his businessman face on. I'm sure it's the one he uses when he fires people and buys out companies. It's cold. Heartless.

This is where he gets his reputation. This is the face and the voice he uses that makes people think he's cruel and motivated only by money. I see it now. He had been so wonderful, I thought maybe the reputation was rumors and jealousy.

I don't think that anymore.

"I mean that none of this is real." His voice is flat. "You were a threat to my brother's relationship. That was a threat to my merger. You wouldn't take money, so I had to deal with it another way. I kept the two of you apart by any means necessary. I had to do something to keep you and Jonathan away from one another. Seducing you was the easiest, most efficient way to get what I wanted."

I thought of our time together on the island. The smiles. The laughs. The way he kissed me. It was all fake. It was all to keep me away from his brother. If I was busy falling in love with Christopher, I wouldn't be able to, or want to, have Jonathan.

It was cruel and twisted.

"Any means necessary?" I repeat, my voice barely making any noise. I shake my head, not wanting to believe what he's saying. "But why go to all this trouble? There has to be easier ways than giving me a resort."

"Because of you and Jonathan last night. I had to stop what was going to happen next. It would ruin everything. I have to get you where Jonathan can't reach you. I knew you wouldn't say no if I said it running a resort for me."

I scoff. "Jonathan told me he wants to be with Adeline. There's no reason for this."

"That's one of Jonathan's dating tricks." Christopher sounds angry. It's a cold anger, something that's been simmering a long time. "It's a way to make you put your guard down. He tells you that he's not interested. Then he says he just can't stay away. That you're all he can think of. That you're the only one who can make him feel this way."

"No." I shake my head, but at the same time I can see Jonathan doing that. It would work. It would make any girl feel special and like she was the only one for him. The way Christopher says it makes me think that he's seen the tactic work one too many times.

"He'll tell you it's love and that it's destined. And after he's had his fun, he'll disappear. He doesn't care about the damage he leaves behind. He doesn't think about the consequences of his actions. It's all about the feeling or right now." Christopher shakes his head. "It's what he does. It's in his nature. He can't help himself."

I think of the way Jonathan's face softened when he mentioned Adeline and I know that this wasn't the case this time. Jonathan loves Adeline. I know he does. He may have said those words to someone else, but he wasn't trying to trick me.

"No," I say. "It's not true. That's not what's happening. You're wrong about him."

"You think so?" Christopher chuckles darkly. It's an unhappy, scoffing sound. "Just after you left him, Jonathan made reservations for a private jet to Las Vegas for two. He ordered the honeymoon suite at the Bellagio."

"So?" My voice cracks a little, but I don't want to believe it. I can't believe it.

"And he set up an Elvis officiant. He wants you to marry him."

CHAPTER 28

Silence fills the room.

I stare at Christopher in complete shock.

"You think that Jonathan is going to whisk me away to Vegas and marry me?" My voice squeaks on the word marry. "He's going to do that after just one conversation and while he has a concussion?"

"He's done more on less," Christopher tells me. "His lawyer is a very wealthy man for a reason."

I take a step away from Christopher. I don't recognize him anymore. He's not the man from the island that made me smile. He's a cold stranger with no love. There's no warmth or sparkle in his eyes.

"So, to keep that from happening, you're sending me away. You're sending me to the islands so he can't even ask me to go with him, even though he's not going to."

"I knew you wouldn't say no if I did it this way." Christopher shrugs like this isn't a big deal. Like he didn't just completely betray me. "I knew you wouldn't ask questions. You would be out of Jonathan's reach and the merger would continue as planned. "

"But you weren't going to come with me? You weren't even going to tell me you would just be late." My hands are trembling so I ball them into fists. "You were going to ditch me?"

"I have a merger to deal with." Anger colors his voice. "I don't have time for you."

His words cut me to the core. I feel my cracked heart start to shatter and it takes everything in me to hold it together. This is what I feared. This is why I didn't let myself fall for him.

But Jonathan said Christopher loved me. I believed him. I thought I had changed Christopher with my love. That a happy ending was possible for him and me.

I am an idiot.

I'm angry with both brothers, but too shocked and heartbroken to know what to do with that anger at the moment.

I've lost both of them. I never really had either of them.

"Was it all a lie? You don't feel anything for me?" I look up at him, blinking away tears that are threatening to come out. My throat is tight and my chest feels like it's going to explode, but my voice stays quiet. I'm surprised at how calm I sound.

"Yes." There is no warmth to his voice. There is no hint of a lie. He looks me in the eye as he says it. The one-word arrow that goes straight to my heart.

I gasp and take an involuntary step backward.

Christopher's face crumples, losing the stern businessman facade. For a moment, there's a hint of the man I knew in the Caribbean. The one that I thought I loved. Hope glimmers for a moment.

"No, that's not entirely true," he admits. The cold, emotionless mask comes back over his face. "I did enjoy our time together. It wasn't unpleasant. You were a good companion."

"Apparently not good enough," I spit at him. Indignation runs hot through my veins. I'm angry and I consider slapping him, but I'm better than that. Instead I dig my nails into my palms as I tighten my fists.

I go to the window and look out at the city. I'm looking but I'm not really seeing. I just don't want to look at Christopher. I wish I could run and hide, but I feel stupid running from his office like a chastised little girl.

I try to collect my thoughts, but they're slippery as fish. I can't focus. My heart is reeling and my head is spinning. I don't understand what is happening. I just keep coming back to our time together, trying to understand how I could have missed this. How he could have tricked me so thoroughly.

There was no clue in his smile. He kissed me like he meant it. The butterflies in my stomach when he said my name were certainly real, but then all that meant was I was a fool. Those butterflies flew on wings of lies.

I'm suddenly very cold. I just want to go home, and I don't mean the apartment above the garage. I need blue water and warm sunshine. White sand beaches and leafy palm trees.

"Was any thing else real?" I ask, turning to face him. "Or was it all just pretend?"

He nods. "You know the answer to that."

The answer is that it was all pretend. And I ate it up, hook, line, and sinker.

I want to run and hide. I want to curl up in a ball and sob. I want to throw the stapler on the desk at his head. I want him to hold me and tell me that everything is okay.

I turn and look out the window again. I don't know what to do now.

I don't want to go home and face my father. I don't want to see Jonathan. I look out across the river and to the ocean. I wish I could simply grow wings and fly across the dark water and find myself back in the place that I feel safe.

I don't want to be here anymore.

"Well, it's a better offer than I expected." I swallow hard, and straighten my spine. I'm better than this. I'm better than him. I won't let him break me. I won't let him see how much he's hurt me. I won't show him how much I could have loved him. How much I did love him. "I accept your offer."

"What offer?" he asks, sounding confused. "We never settled on a number."

"I'll take the hotel and the plane ride to get to it," I tell him, lifting my chin. This isn't what I want, but I'm going to take what I can get. I'm not a complete idiot. Just a big one.

I walk calmly to the table and pick up the files. I sign the last page with a flourish and hand it to him.

"Do I need to do anything special for the plane?" I ask. "Or were they only expecting me tomorrow anyway?"

"They were expecting only you," he says. His voice is softer now, but I don't care. I don't care about him anymore.

I give a curt nod and turn on my heel. I pick up my bag from the table and walk out of the room. I'm not going to let him see me cry. He doesn't deserve even that much.

I make it to the elevator before I burst into tears. At least he can't see me there.

CHAPTER 29

It's almost dark when I get home. The sun hangs low in the sky, casting an orange warmth that makes everything look ruddy and joyful. I don't feel it, though.

I half expect my dad to be sitting out on the front porch waiting for me. The light is on his room, so I assume he's in bed reading. I'm glad. I don't want to talk to him. I don't want to tell him he was right about Christopher.

Just thinking about it hurts.

I need a drink.

I know there's some bottles of champagne still in the kitchen from a recent party. The supplier will come and get the extras at the end of the week. The Lewis family ordered and already paid for all of them, so taking one isn't a problem. My dad often saves one or two in the fridge with Deborah's blessing.

I sneak into the kitchen. The main house is dark and quiet except for the hum of the air conditioners. Deborah and Christopher are still at the office working, so they aren't home. I'm not sure where Jonathan is, but I'd probably guess he's either at his apartment or halfway to Vegas.

Either way, the staff has gone home and the place is deserted. I'm able to sneak in and find a bottle without any trouble. I pop the cork and take a sip right from the bottle. It's good and bubbly.

I look down at the label and start to laugh. I'm drinking Cristal Champagne from the bottle like a college frat boy. I'm so classy.

I take the bottle and go outside. It's too cold in the kitchen with the air conditioning. Besides, my thoughts are swirling and I just want to go somewhere peaceful. Somewhere I can think.

I go to the bench by the koi pond. The big weeping willow tree moves slightly in the gentle breeze. The koi pond ripples as the fish swim by and the water glitters in the setting sun. I take another gulp straight from the bottle, lean back, and close my eyes. I'm starting to feel a light buzz that I'm hoping will start to numb the pain in my heart.

"You know, I'm supposed to be here for this. This is kind of my champagne drinking spot."

I open my eyes to see Jonathan standing in front of me with a smile on his face.

He's in comfortable looking shorts and a t-shirt. He looks just as handsome as I always imagine him. The sun warms his hair and sparkles in his eyes.

"Mind if I join you?" he asks me, motioning to the empty spot beside me.

I take another gulp of champagne. "I didn't bring a second glass."

He shrugs. "I brought my own." He pulls out a flask

from his back pocket and I nod to him. I scoot over to give him a little more room.

We sit for a moment, not saying anything. The sun is gold and red, the pond glitters, and the only sound is the splash of the fountain.

It would be peaceful if not for my broken heart.

Jonathan sits beside me, all masculine energy and sexiness. I don't want him. The irony of this isn't lost on me. Two weeks ago, I would have given my left hand to be sitting on this bench alone with Jonathan. This would have made me the happiest woman in the world.

Today, I just want to crawl into a hole and die. My heart is broken and not even Jonathan can fix it.

"Why are we drinking?" Jonathan asks, taking a small sip from his flask. "Drinking to remember or drinking to forget?"

"I should be celebrating," I reply. I did just get a new hotel. That's something worthy of opening a bottle of Cristal.

Jonathan raises his eyebrows. "You don't look like you're celebrating."

"You were wrong about him." I take another gulp of champagne. "Christopher doesn't love me."

"He wouldn't know love if it bit him on the ass." Jonathan sighs. "I'm sorry."

We both drink.

"I hear you're going to Vegas." I take another sip of champagne. I'm definitely feeling it now. I've had half the bottle and nothing to eat since the one bite of sandwich.

Jonathan looks over at me in surprise. "How'd you hear that?"

"Three guesses." I take another gulp. I'm determined to

numb the pain with this bottle. "He was sure you were going to ask me. I told him you weren't."

"It's not for another two days. That bastard." Jonathan shakes his head. He takes a breath before looking over at me. "I hate to disappoint you, but it's not for you. I'm asking Adeline to elope with me."

"I figured." I hold out the bottle. "Cheers to that. Congratulations."

He clinks his flask against my bottle. We both take a drink. His sip is small and delicate. I take half the bottle.

"What made you take the jump?" I ask him. I don't look at him. I look out at the koi pond. The glimmer of sunset on the water is mesmerizing.

"I love her," he tells me with a shrug. "I'm going to marry her before I lose my nerve."

"That sounds very romantic," I tell him with just a hint of sarcasm in my voice.

He chuckles. "You know me better than most. What do you think?"

I set my bottle to the side and twist at the waist to look at him. His eyes are serious. They're a shade lighter than Christopher's. His hair is lighter too, probably from being out in the sun. Jonathan's hair is cut in a fashionable style where Christopher is utilitarian. I realize that I now compare Jonathan to Christopher rather than Christopher to Jonathan. Christopher is my new benchmark for a man.

Lucky me.

"Tell me you love her," I say. I watch his face, looking for any hint that he doesn't mean it.

"I love her. I love Adeline." The corners of his mouth smile when he says her name. His eyes go distant and soft. There's an easy set to his shoulders that I haven't seen before. He's comfortable in his own skin, with a peace within him that he hasn't had before.

"You do love her," I say. There's a little sadness in my voice, but more from lost opportunity than actual remorse. I'm genuinely happy for him and besides, I love someone else now. "She's a lucky lady."

"You think so?" he asks, looking a little surprised.

"Yup." I nod. "But maybe skip the Elvis impersonator marrying you. Unless she's into Elvis, there are more traditional options, even in Vegas."

"Good point. I'll keep it in mind," he says with a smile.

I take another chug of champagne. My bottle is almost gone. "I'm leaving tomorrow. That's where the 'should be celebrating' comes from. I got a job."

"Where?" Jonathan asks, sounding a little sad. That makes me feel a little wanted at least.

"Back to the Caribbean. It's my dream job." I don't tell him the specifics of it. I don't tell him that it's his brother's payment to keep me away. I don't tell him what it cost me.

"So soon?" Jonathan asks. "What about your dad?"

"He'll be fine here." I wish I could stay a little bit longer, but I know my dad will be fine. Besides, I don't think I can stay here. Not any more.

"I'm impressed you got a job so quickly," Jonathan says. I notice that he's put his flask away.

"I'm actually pretty good at what I do. I'm highly sought after." Kind of. I didn't actually get this job on merit, but I'm not going to let that stop me.

"That is a true statement. You are definitely sought after," Jonathan says. He smiles at me and even though I don't love him anymore, he still makes my heart flutter.

"Thanks." I take another gulp of champagne. Soon, I hope I won't feel much anymore.

We sit for a moment, just watching the sunset in comfortable silence.

"I'm sorry I was wrong about my brother," Jonathan says after a while. "I often am with him. Is he the reason you're leaving?"

"A little." That's the understatement of the year. "But it's also what I should do. It's a good career move for me."

"Well, congratulations. I hope it works out for you."

"Thank you." I finish off my champagne and set the empty bottle to the side. "And good luck to you in Las Vegas."

He grins as he stands up. "I've already won."

He leans over and gives me a kiss on the cheek. His lips are soft on my skin, but the kiss is short and sweet. It's brotherly and kind.

I watch him walk into the sunset and out of my life. I sit for a moment, letting the numbness of the alcohol seep into my bones. I stare out at the koi pond, wondering how my life got here.

I can't help but chuckle as I realize that I finally had champagne and a kiss with Jonathan. Yet one more dream come true.

CHAPTER 30

I drink fizzy lemonade the entire way to the island.

I do add a little vodka, but it still counts as mostly lemonade.

Dad drove me to the airport just before lunch. I didn't tell him about Christopher. I just told him that I'd gotten this amazing job opportunity and that I was taking it. I think he was actually glad I was leaving the Lewis boys behind. He promised to come visit me soon.

He gave me a hug and told me he was proud of me. I cried. He cried. And I got on the plane and drank lemonade and vodka.

The island comes into view as we circle around and prepare to land. I look out the window and will my heart to mend. The blue waters, white sand beaches, and warm sun will do wonders for my mental health. I keep telling myself that once I'm back on an island and working, I'll forget all about Christopher.

It didn't work that way for Jonathan, but I keep telling myself that it might work for Christopher anyway.

"More lemonade?" the stewardess asks, coming over with a full glass.

I shake my head. "How soon until we land?"

"We have to circle around again. There's another plane with priority landing," she explains.

I nod and she goes to the back area again. I wonder who could possibly be more important than the Lewis family jet. Even though I'm the one on the jet, as far as anyone else knows there are billionaires on board.

I try to relax and just enjoy the view outside the window as the pilot does his job and circles us around the island again. I'm trying not to think of Christopher, and it's next to impossible, especially while I'm riding in his airplane.

I see things all around that I want to show him. I see the deep water and want to tell him about the whales. I see my drink on the table and remember that he drinks sparkling water on these flights. I know that once we get to the resort, it's going to be more of the same.

I will see him everywhere I go, and yet know that he isn't there. That he never really was. That our relationship was all in my head. It was no different than my relationship with Jonathan, except that Christopher participated this time. Still, the emotions were all in my head. They weren't real for him. Christopher didn't feel anything for me. Jonathan didn't feel anything for me.

It's best that I'm going to live here on the island. Maybe I can finally find someone that loves me and have the relationship actually exist. Maybe I can finally bring someone home to meet my dad. Maybe they'll meet Jonathan and Christopher.

Maybe he can punch Christopher for me.

Maybe Christopher will be married by then. Maybe we'll all be loved.

I would like that.

Despite it all, I hope that Christopher is happy.

Well, I hope that he's miserable right now. Eventually he can be happy. Maybe in ten years. That feels generous enough.

The plane lands with a soft thud. We taxi down the runway and pull to a stop. I step out through the door and take a deep breath of humid island air.

I'm home.

The humidity is different here than it is in New York City. It's cleaner and feels almost softer. There's a warmth and a joy to the air here that doesn't exist anywhere else but on the islands. There's a magic to it.

I don't ride in a limo this time. I'm not a guest, so they don't send the fancy car to come get me. I'm here to work. Instead of a limo, I take a cab. I only brought a couple of suitcases, so it's not hard to get off the airplane and into the car. I'll have a small apartment in the staff housing unit that's fully furnished, so all I need is clothes. I'll purchase some new work things once I know better what to expect.

The drive is slower this time. I don't know if it's because I'm by myself or if it's the cab and I'm just uncomfortable. I play on my phone, looking at photos of the resort. The on-site housing is off to the side and away from the guests. There are no amazing views from the building, but it will still be nice to be near the ocean.

Besides, I'm not here for the view. I'm here to work. I'm here to run this hotel and make it even better. This wasn't my plan but I'm going to make sure this place succeeds. It's how I'll get over this.

The cab drops me off in front of the entrance to the hotel. Yet again, I'm struck with memories of Christopher. I've known him my whole life. I've loved him for a week. The life part only makes the week feel like more.

If I had known last week what I know now, I would have guarded my heart better. I wouldn't have believed Jonathan. I would still have come here though. I would have still slept with him. I would have done everything the same, because it was a beautiful experience.

I wouldn't have told him how I felt. I wouldn't have let him into my heart. If I had known, I probably would just have a very intense crush on Christopher rather than full on love. The crush would be survivable. I'd lived with crushes before.

This heartache though, of letting myself love and finding out it was all fake, that killed my confidence and my dreams.

I stand in front of the entrance for a moment, bags in hand.

This is my new life.

It will be a good life. I don't need Christopher. I didn't need him before. I did just fine living without Jonathan and I'll do just as well without Christopher.

Christopher doesn't love me. He could have decided to finish the merger and come out and join me and I never would have known the difference. At least not for a while. He could have kept up the charade.

Instead, he went scorched earth and made sure I would never come back. He hurt me on purpose. I ran away from him and fled New York.

I guess that's one way to keep me away from Jonathan. Did he really think I was that big of a threat? The idea of me as some sort of seductress, tempting every man and making them fall wildly in love with me is amusing. Ridiculous, but amusing. I can barely tempt a cat with a can of tuna.

I take a deep breath and pick up my bags. I can do this. I can have a good life here. I can forget him. It was only a couple of days that we were really a couple. The time we spent together growing up doesn't count.

It obviously didn't mean anything to him.

I push back tears. I'm not going to be weak. I am strong. Christopher Lewis can go suck on a lemon. He can go jump in a lake. He can get eaten by a shark for all I care.

I straighten my shoulders and go inside.

Cool air blows against my skin making me shiver after the warmth of the tropical sun outside. The lobby feels peaceful.

There is a different woman at the desk than last time. I smile at her and walk over.

"Hi. I'm Nora Bailey."

"Welcome to the Ocean Retreat," the woman replies. "How may I help you?"

"I'm a new manager," I tell her. I pull out a printed off email with all my information. "Can you show me where employee housing is?"

The woman takes the paper and frowns at it. "This is really embarrassing," she says, her cheeks darkening. "I have no idea what this is. I'm going to need to check with my manager."

"Oh?" How could she not know where employee housing was? Did she not live there too?

"I'm so sorry. I'm used to just checking in guests." She

picks up the phone and gives me a nervous smile. "I'll call her right away."

I go and take a seat in one of the comfy lobby chairs. My foot taps as I wait for her to finish speaking with her manager.

"It'll just be a moment, ma'am," the desk clerk tells me. "My manager is with a guest at the moment. I apologize again."

I nod and wait. I look around the room, taking in the fans and artwork. The chair is comfy, but I really just want to get to my room and settle in. I want a shower. I want a nap. I'm still a little hung over from the champagne last night and the vodka on the plane has completely worn off. I am not a happy camper.

I'm not a guest, but this isn't good hotel etiquette.

This is something we're going to work on if this is going to be my hotel. I want my employees to be ready for anything. I want them to be ready for everything. The response "I have to ask my manager" will be only for emergencies, and in those rare cases, I want a manager at the desk in two seconds.

I check my watch to see that ten minutes have passed. My foot taps harder.

At the fifteen minute mark I get up and go back to the desk.

"Any updates?" I ask her. No other guests have checked in so it's not like she has a lot to do.

"She should be here any minute," the clerk assures me. She looks nervous. I hope that the manger gets here soon. This is unacceptable in my hotel.

"You really can't tell me where employee housing is?" I ask her, annoyance filling my voice.

"Oh, here's the manager," the clerk tells me, relief flooding her face. She runs across the lobby to the woman who checked me in last time I was here.

"Anna, this is Ms. Bailey," the clerk tells her. "She says she needs employee housing."

"Ms. Bailey, I remember you," Anna says warmly. She smiles and shakes my hand. "I am so sorry for the confusion. We don't get many new employees. I know it's not the best introduction to a new owner, but I'm afraid it couldn't be helped."

"I really just want to go to my room," I tell her. I can feel a headache starting behind my eyes.

"Of course, I completely understand." She goes behind the desk and I have to stifle the urge to shout at her. She sees my face and smiles politely again. "I just need to check the computer to see which building you need."

I cross my arms and try to keep my annoyance in check. This feels like stalling, but for what reason, I have no idea. Either way, both of these women are currently on my "do I want to keep this employee or not" list.

"If you'll follow me," Anna says, coming out from behind the desk. "I'll take your suitcase. It's the least I can do."

I hand her my bigger bag without any guilt. The small one I pull behind me as I follow Anna across the lobby. It's the same way we went when I was a guest. She even goes out on the boardwalk again, leading out to the guest bungalows.

"Where are we going?" I ask her. "This can't be the way to staff housing."

"You're right. It's not," Anna tells me. But she just

keeps walking, taking my suitcase with her. I have no choice but to follow.

"What the heck?" I say under my breath. I stare at her back for a moment, trying to figure out what in the world she is doing. I have some serious employee training to work on.

I catch up to Anna outside the bungalow that Christopher and I shared. There are no more rooms after this, so this is obviously where she wants me to be. I don't want to go in that door though. I don't want to remember my happy time with Christopher. Not today.

"I can't stay here," I tell her. "This is for guests. I'm not a guest."

"Your employee housing is unavailable," Anna informs me. She motions to the door. "This room is. It's the only one on the island for you right now."

"This room?" I shake my head. Of course it's this room. Of course the only freaking room available on the entire freaking island.

Anna is so fired.

"Fine." I snatch my bag out of her hand and push open the door. I'm already figuring out the worst possible schedule that I can put her on for this. It's petty and I know it, but staying in heartbreak room was not what I needed today.

I step inside and all thoughts go straight out of my head.

The entire bungalow is filled with flowers. Roses, orchids, lilies, jasmine and more fill every table and all the floor space.

"What the..." I turn to ask Anna what's going on, but she's closing the door and hurrying away.

I turn back around, looking at the room full of flowers in absolute stunned confusion.

And then I see him.

He has a bouquet of roses in his hands. I missed him the first time because they act as camouflage against all the other flowers in the room.

Christopher.

CHAPTER 31

My heart stalls.

Shock, anger, love, hate, surprise, and then combinations of those each try to take control, but none of them seem to know which emotion should be in charge. I stare at him, my mouth open and jaw on the floor.

I now see why the desk clerk didn't want to take me to employee housing. I'm tempted to change my mind about firing her and Anna. They did good customer service by stalling, even if it was helping Christopher.

Why is he here, though? Is this some kind of sick joke? I consider slugging him, but I don't know what good that would do.

He takes a step forward.

"I'm sorry, Nora."

I cross my arms. He doesn't get to break my heart and then just apologize and make everything better. I don't care how many flowers he brings. "What are you doing here?"

"Apologizing." He swallows hard and takes another

step toward me, his eyes focused intently on me. "And if that doesn't work, I'm willing to beg for your forgiveness."

My feet grow roots to the floor. It's a good thing because I feel like a stiff breeze could knock me over. Those roots are the only thing keeping me standing.

"What do you want, Christopher?" My voice is cold. I'm not sure what to do with the rising hope in my chest. It's a traitorous feeling. I should be angry, not hopeful.

He takes another step toward me. He's wearing the same pants as yesterday, but a different shirt. Even though it's new, there are wrinkles all over it. His hair is a mess. His eyes are red, like he has been crying. He definitely hasn't slept in days.

"I want you, Nora."

It takes a lot of strength, but I pull up the roots holding me in place to take a step away from him.

"You had me. You didn't want me."

"I know." He sighs, lowering the flowers. "I'm an idiot. I was wrong. I'm sorry."

I've never heard Christopher say those words. He's a high powered billionaire that owns a major corporation. He's never wrong. He never has to apologize, or at least he never has to mean it. But he means it now.

He's not a billionaire right now. He's just a man.

"Keep going," I tell him, my arms still crossed. "You hurt me."

"And for that, I'll never forgive myself." He looks up at me, his blue eyes full of regret. "I was afraid."

"Afraid?" I scoff. "Afraid of what?"

"Of happiness." A bitter smile dances across his face and he winces and touches his eye.

I evaluate him for a moment. I don't think this is a

trick. There's no reason to trick me anymore. Still, I'm angry. He hurt me. He lied to me. He tricked me.

"What changed your mind?" I ask.

A small smile crosses his face. "Someone you've heard a lot about, but never met."

I think about it for a moment. "Adeline?"

"Jonathan went to her last night and told her everything. *Everything*," he says with emphasis. "From your first meeting at the bar to your last night meeting at the house."

"What does she care?" I ask. "Jonathan probably told the story like I was a homewrecker."

Christopher shakes his head. "But he didn't. He told Adeline about his last minute jitters. The thoughts he had. He confessed it all, and how much he regretted hurting two good people in his life."

I whistle. Maybe there's some hope for Jonathan yet.

"But she had to hear it from me. So she came to my office. There, she found me hugging a bottle and crying. A pretty sad sight. Much like you were, I guess."

"So she decided to play matchmaker to make us both happy?" I ask.

"Not for us, and maybe not even for Jonathan." Christopher smiles, as if something finally makes sense to him. "But she really cares about her company. She told me to get my head together so that we could complete this merger and I could concentrate on what was important."

"So you jumped on a plane and headed here because she gave you a pep talk?"

"Nope," he says, then laughs. "I told her the same thing. It's impossible. I don't have time. It's better this way."

I cross my arms. This wasn't the apology I was expecting.

"So she tells me that if I went this far to make sure the merger went through, that I'd make a vacation work. And that if I didn't go here to make this right, the merger was off."

I gasp. "Do you think she would?"

"Oh, I know she would. Even after she said that, I called her bluff. She called her secretary and started making plans right in front of me."

I didn't know what to think. "So, are you here because of the merger, or are you here because you love me?"

Christopher smiles, and it's the warmest smile I've ever seen from him. "I came here to save the merger, but standing in front of you right now, I know the answer to this question. And you know it, too."

He crosses the distance to me. He throws his bouquet of flowers to one side before wrapping his arms around me in a big hug. "I love you, Nora." Christopher's eyes come to mine. "I was fool not to realize it. I'd cancel this business deal right now to keep you. It took my brother's fiance playing business games to realize what I'd done to you. To us."

My heart is pounding in my chest. He loves me. Christopher Lewis loves me. He was willing to blow a billion dollars to make me happy.

He takes a step forward and I don't retreat this time.

"I love you, Nora. And I'm sorry I ever made you think otherwise." He looks down at the flowers in his hand. "I don't deserve you. But I want to try and make you happy."

I stand in shocked silence for a moment.

"Oh, Christopher." I go to him, putting my hand to his

cheek. There's stubble there, indicating what a mess he is. He always shaves in the morning. He looks at me with big blue eyes that would melt my heart even if he wasn't confessing his love.

"Please tell me I haven't lost my chance," he says. His voice cracks.

I smile and go to my tip toes. I plant a soft kiss on his lips. "You have lost your chance," I whisper. I smile up at him. "But you can have another one."

A shuddering breath runs through him and he wraps his arms around me. I hug him tightly. He brings his fingers to my chin and draws me into his kiss.

"I love you," I whisper. He kisses me more passion-ately, as if I'm oxygen and he's been trapped underwater.

Caribbean sunshine has nothing on the warmth of his kiss. The beauty of the sea and the sky pale in comparison to how he makes me feel. There is nothing in the world as warm and bright as love. There is no where I would rather be than in Christopher's arms. He is the brother I choose.

T *en months later*

This hospital is freezing. You'd think since it's snowing outside they'd heat the building more, but no. I feel like I can practically see my breath every time I exhale.

"Why is it so cold in here?" I ask Christopher.

He smiles and shrugs out of his jacket. "Here."

He wraps his suit jacket around my shoulders. Even through my sweater, I can feel his warmth seep into me.

I smile up at him. He grins. I love that he smiles more now. His skin is sun-kissed and he needs a haircut. He still shaves every morning, but sometimes he will skip a day or two just because he can. He shaved today because today is important.

Today, we met his nephew.

Deborah paces the waiting room, looking anxious and

excited at the same time. She keeps checking her watch and mumbling about the time.

The door opens to the hospital suite and we all perk up.

"It's a boy!" Jonathan announces. He's grinning from ear to ear. I thought he had looked happy in the pictures of his elopement. I thought he had looked happy when we visited him at the office, but this makes that joy seem mild.

This is joy that radiates through the soul.

Jonathan goes back inside and Deborah, Christopher and I all start chattering about how wonderful it is the baby is here.

"Soon, that will be us," Christopher whispers, kissing the side of head.

"How many kids should we have?" I ask, looking down at the ring on my finger. Our wedding is just a few months away. We plan to have it in the spring on the island.

"At least two," he says, a thoughtful look on his face. "They each need a sibling like I need Jonathan."

"You didn't need him for a long time," I say.

"I didn't know that I needed him," Christopher corrects. "But I wouldn't be able to run the company without him now. I wouldn't be able to be with you the way we are now."

"That's true," I agree. I like that Christopher has been in the Caribbean with me.

When Christopher came to the Caribbean to get me back, Jonathan took over running the company. He finished the merger. It helped that Adeline insisted upon it. What Adeline says is law around here. So Christopher went on vacation while Jonathan ran things.

It was the first vacation Christopher had ever taken.

Jonathan did phenomenally. The company is thriving. And having two CEOs that are intent on creating the best business possible means that the workload between them is shared. Jonathan has a purpose and Christopher no longer carries the burden by himself.

The business is truly a family business again.

My father retired after Christmas. With Christopher in the Caribbean and Jonathan with a household of his own, there was no reason for Deborah to need all the staff. She kept the house, but now just has enough staff to keep things running.

My father moved to the islands and lives just a few miles away from me. He's finally learning to relax again himself. I don't worry about him as much anymore.

And now that Jonathan has a son, Christopher will go back to managing some of the business again. We'll be traveling back and forth between New York and the Caribbean as we need to. I have a feeling Christopher will be less stressed this time around. He knows how to relax now. Business and money are no longer all that his world is made of.

He now knows love.

And so do I.

Jonathan comes out with a small bundle in his arms. Pride beams off his face as he introduces his son to us. "James Paxton Lewis," he tells us. "After Dad."

I see tears form in Christopher's eyes as he takes the baby from his brother. He looks so right with a baby in his arms. He smiles down at the boy and my ovaries nearly explode.

"Hello, James," Christopher whispers. "Welcome to the family."

He grins at me and I grin back. Christopher carefully passes the infant to me.

James is so small and delicate I can hardly believe he's real. He's perfect as he sleeps, snuggled up in his blankets. I look down at him and I'm once again, I'm completely in love with a Lewis boy.

I look to Christopher and see my future shining bright.

The man I love is getting married.
And it's to me.
I've been in love with Christopher Lewis for as long as I can remember without knowing it.
I loved him as a girl.
I loved him as a teenager.
I loved him as an adult.
I love him still.
And he loves me.

An American Cinderella: A Royal Love Story

"I'd give up my whole kingdom to be with you. I want to be your Prince Charming."

Aria has a big heart but bigger problems. Her whole life is a mess thanks to her controlling stepmother. But when she's knocked over- literally- by the hottest man she's ever had the pleasure of tangling up her body with, everything changes.

Henry Prescott, second-string rugby player for the Paradisa Royals, is funny, sweet, charming, and oh-so-sexy. He's got a rock hard body and tackles her in bed as fiercely as he tackled her in the park. Knowing nothing about rugby, but absolutely intoxicated by his accent, she finds herself falling for him.

There's only one problem: Henry Prescott doesn't exist.

The man she thinks she loves is actually Prince Henry, second in line for the throne of the nation of Paradisa. He's the man who Aria's entire department has to impress for trade relations. And that makes Aria's stepmother's plans even more dangerous.

He's the man who could destroy her world or make all her dreams come true.

He lied about being a prince... did he also lie about being in love?

NYT Bestseller Krista Lakes brings you this brand new sweet-and-sexy royal romance. This standalone novel will have you cheering for an American princess's happily ever after.

An American Cinderella: A Royal Love Story

ABOUT THE AUTHOR

New York Times and USA Today Bestseller Krista Lakes is a thirtysomething who recently rediscovered her passion for writing. She is living happily ever after with her Prince Charming. Her first kid just started preschool and she is happy to welcome her second child into her life, continuing her "Happily Ever After"!

Thank you for supporting an indie author. Anything you can do, whether it be writing a review, or even simply telling a fellow reader that you enjoyed this, helps me out immensely. Thanks!

Krista would love to hear from you! Please contact her at Krista.Lakes@gmail.com or friend her on Facebook!

Further reading:

Bad Boys and Babies
    Family Doctor's Baby
    The Billionaire's Baby Arrangement
    Crime Boss Baby

Kinds of Love
    A Forever Kind of Love
    A Wonderful Kind of Love

An Endless Kind of Love

Billionaires and Brides
Yours Completely: A Cinderella Love Story
Yours Truly: A Cinderella Love Story
Yours Royally: A Cinderella Love Story

The "Kisses" series
Saltwater Kisses: A Billionaire Love Story
Kisses From Jack: The Other Side of Saltwater Kisses
Rainwater Kisses: A Billionaire Love Story
Champagne Kisses: A Timeless Love Story
Freshwater Kisses: A Billionaire Love Story
Sandcastle Kisses: A Billionaire Love Story
Hurricane Kisses: A Billionaire Love Story
Barefoot Kisses: A Billionaire Love Story
Sunrise Kisses: A Billionaire Love Story
Waterfall Kisses: A Billionaire Love Story
Island Kisses: A Billionaire Love Story

Other Novels
I Choose You: A Secret Billionaire Romance
His Every Desire: A Billionaire Seduction
Wolf Six's Salvation: A Shifter Love Story
Burned: A New Adult Love Story
Walking on Sunshine: A Sweet Summer Romance
An American Cinderella: A Royal Love Story
Mr. Darcy's Kiss: A Contemporary Pride and Prejudice